W9-BFF-438

William Marshall has worked as a journalist, teacher, proof-reader, mortuary attendant, process worker and playwright. Born in Sydney, Australia, in 1944, he has since lived in Hong Kong, Switzerland, Wales and Ireland before returning to Australia in 1983 with his wife and daughter.

The first novel in William Marshall's Yellowthread Street series, *Yellowthread Street*, is also available from Futura.

Also by William Marshall

YELLOWTHREAD STREET

WILLIAM MARSHALL

The Far Away Man

A Yellowthread Street Mystery

Futura

A *Futura* Book

Copyright © William Marshall 1984

First published in Great Britain in 1984
by Martin Secker & Warburg Ltd

This edition published in 1987
by Futura Publications, a Division of
Macdonald & Co (Publishers) Ltd
London & Sydney

ISBN 0 7088 2728 4

Printed and bound in Great Britain by
Collins, Glasgow

Futura Publications
A Division of
Macdonald & Co (Publishers) Ltd
Greater London House
Hampstead Road
London NW1 7QX

A BPCC plc Company

The Hong Bay district of Hong Kong is fictitious, as are the people who, for one reason or another, inhabit it.

MR MUI

Jade possesses the five major virtues which man should strive for. By its warmth and bright lustre it typifies charity. Because of its translucence it reveals its inner faults and typifies sincerity.

When struck, it sends out a note which is pure and so typifies wisdom. Jade can be broken but never bent; thus it typifies courage.

Though it might have sharp edges it will not harm; thus it typifies intelligence . . .

Outside Mr Mui's Chinese jade shop on Wyang Street, Hong Bay, the world on a torrid Hong Kong midsummer's morning was going about its business. Inside, it was coming to an end.

Mr Mui, with gravel in his stomach, said desperately in English, 'Don't you even sweat? The air conditioning isn't on. It's as hot as hell in here. Don't you even *sweat*?'

He looked hard at The Far Away Man facing him across his glass-topped counter. The Far Away Man's forehead was clear. He didn't sweat. The Far Away Man looked like a tall, thin European display mannequin. In the entire half-hour he had been standing in the shop with his back to the street he had said not one syllable. Mr Mui said, 'I've never done anything in my life to deserve this!' Mr Mui's voice changed into a shout, 'I've never cheated you! *I don't even know you!*'

Mr Mui's hands were palm down on the glass top of his counter. The hands were shaking. Mr Mui said, 'Talk to me!' His voice was rising, 'Look, in all my life I can't think of one thing I've –' Mr Mui said, 'Talk to me!' He lifted his hands.

The gun in The Far Away Man's hand made a click.

Mr Mui said, 'All right!' He lowered his hands, 'All right.'

The Far Away Man's eyes were pale blue and expressionless. Mr Mui said soothingly, 'Look, I understand there's a gulf between us: between Europeans and Chinese – a gulf in business methods, but if I cheated you at some time it wasn't meant. How could I have cheated you this much? What have I got in the shop that I could have cheated you on that's worth a life?' He looked around anxiously at his stock. There was nothing. Mr Mui said, 'Look, I'm just a middle-range retailer. I'm bonded by the Hong Kong Tourist Association. If you feel that I cheated you on the price of something all you have to do is complain to them!' The gravel in his stomach had formed into a moving quarry wall of lava. He felt it burn at his ulcer. Mr Mui said, 'Look, it's 8 a.m., there's no money in the shop. I shouldn't even be open.' He tried to see into the eyes, but they were far away, not even seeing him. Mr Mui said, 'I came down because I thought maybe you wanted something before you caught a plane or something! A gift. I was being kind!' Mr Mui said – Mr Mui said softly, 'Please don't kill me.'

Outside, a knot of schoolchildren went by the shop on their way to early morning summer classes. Mr Mui's eyes followed them. One of them reminded him of his daughter when she had been at the same school. Mr Mui looked down at his hands on the glass counter. They were outlined in sweat. He saw The Far Away Man's pale blue eyes narrow slightly as he twisted his head to follow the schoolchildren. There seemed to be something at the corner of his mouth: a spot of something dark. The Far Away Man wiped it away with his free hand.

Mr Mui said, 'I'm not going to move!' He forced himself to look at the muzzle of the gun. 'That isn't a small gun. You shoot that in here and someone will hear. I'm not moving so if you think you're going to get me into the back room or upstairs

2

so you can –' Mr Mui said, 'You're wrong! I'm not moving. I'm staying here!'

Mr Mui knew almost nothing about guns, but he knew enough to know that the long barrelled pistol pointing at him held only one shot. It was a killer's gun.

'This is insane! What are you waiting for?' Mr Mui said at the end of argument, 'I'm not some sort of dog you kill without even a pat on the head! I'm a man like you!' Mr Mui said, '*Talk to me!*'

The Far Away Man's eyes came back to him slowly. It was a spot of blood on his mouth. Mr Mui tried to work out how old he was. Forty-five? Fifty? It was almost impossible to tell with Europeans. He looked for some human connection between them. There was nothing. He felt his stomach turn over, his blood thumping in his heart, a pulse in his neck going: all the things of life.

He looked at The Far Away Man. There was nothing. He was like a dummy, a statue, something filled with rags, not alive, not dead, just –

Mr Mui said, 'My daughter got married the other day.' He felt the tears welling up. Mr Mui said, 'I refused to go to her wedding. I'm not talking to her.' There was a squeaking sound. He looked down and saw it was his hands rubbing on the glass counter top. 'If you kill me now she'll think I died still disapproving of her! I expected years more of life to forgive her, to –' Mr Mui said, 'I'm only punishing her because she hurt me! If you kill me now she'll think –' Mr Mui said quietly, 'She'll think I didn't love her!' He fell silent for a moment. Mr Mui said desperately, 'Aren't you human? Don't you have –'

The gun came up and there was a single, loud, readying click.

Mr Mui said calmly, 'I want to go to the toilet. I don't care if I have to piss in one of the jade bowls over there, but I want to relieve myself before you kill me.' There was a muscle twitching at the corner of his mouth. Mr Mui said, 'I demand that much. That's what my life's going to cost you and I insist on the price without negotiation.' He looked hard at The Far Away Man's pale eyes. Mr Mui said, 'I'll make it easy for you. I'll go into a room out of sight of the street, but in return I want to relieve myself. You can leave me that much. Whatever I've done to you, you can recover by killing me, but my body won't mean anything to you when I'm dead, but it will mean something to my family and I don't want them to see me with piss running out of my trousers like some derelict old man. That's my bargain.' Mr Mui said, 'It's a fair one.' He shook his head, 'Whatever you think, I've never cheated you.' Mr Mui said, 'All I ask is that you kill me man to man.'

Someone came to the shop window. The Far Away Man's eyes flickered to him. It was a shoe shine man setting up early morning business in the doorway.

Mr Mui looked at the gun. It stared at him uncomprehendingly. Above it The Far Away Man's eyes were far away, not there, looking but not seeing.

The Far Away Man tensed.

It was all over with him, with the eyes and the face. Now it was only the gun.

Mr Mui saw its black muzzle staring at him. The barrel came up. There was a soft click as The Far Away Man drew back the hammer.

It was just the gun.

Mr Mui felt his bladder reach bursting point. If his hands were moving on the glass counter top he could no longer feel them. He felt his stomach move. A sound came out of him. Across his shoulder blades something was drawing tight, crushing in his chest.

Mr Mui said –

He thought, "I'm going to piss. I'm going to die in the middle of pissing and it'll go on after I'm dead and I'll be found here stinking in the hot weather like some sort of –"

The Far Away Man was moving, going towards the door so that after Mr Mui was dead, after the world had come to an end for him, his daughter would continue living and thinking and –

4

Mr Mui said in a shriek, 'In the name of Heaven, *don't you even have a single doubt?*'

The Far Away Man's eyes were looking at him.

The Far Away Man said so softly as to be almost inaudible, 'No, none at all.'

In the doorway the shoe shine man looked up as The Far Away Man opened the door to the street.

For an instant, The Far Away Man's eyes and the gun muzzle were one, looking across the shop floor at Mr Mui. Mr Mui said –

The pale eyes, for an instant, seemed alive. They blinked. Mr Mui saw a pulse in The Far Away Man's neck, like his own. He saw a single spot of blood. He saw –

He saw the shoe shine man look up as the door opened beside him. He saw him start to get up. He saw The Far Away Man, still looking across the shop, put a hand on the shoe shine man's shoulder to restrain him. He saw –

He felt time.

He *felt* it. Time. Like a gift; minutes, hours, days, weeks, years: a *lifetime*. He felt it. He felt it given. He –

In the doorway, still looking at Mr Mui, The Far Away Man, without emotion or change, put the muzzle of the pistol against the shoe shine man's ear and pulled the trigger.

Hong Kong is an island of some thirty square miles under British administration in the South China Sea facing the Kowloon and New Territories area of continental China. Kowloon and the New Territories are also British administered, surrounded by the Communist Chinese province of Kwangtung. The climate is generally sub-tropical, with hot, humid summers and heavy rainfall. The population of Hong Kong and the surrounding areas at any one time, including tourists and visitors, is in excess of five millions. The New Territories are leased from the Chinese. The lease is due to expire in 1997, but the British nevertheless maintain a military presence along the border, although, should the Communists, who supply almost all the colony's drinking water, ever desire

5

to terminate the lease early, they need only turn off the taps. Hong Bay is on the southern side of the island and the tourist brochures advise you not to go there after dark.

Jade possesses the five major virtues which man should strive for. By its warmth and bright lustre it typifies charity. Because of its translucence it reveals its inner faults and typifies sincerity.

When struck, it sends out a note which is pure and so typifies wisdom. Jade can be broken but never bent; thus it typifies courage.

Though it may have sharp edges it will not harm, thus it typifies intelligence . . .

In his shop, Mr Mui, with every ounce of self control he possessed, went slowly and carefully towards the back room to the toilet.

There were no thoughts in his mind. He simply made it one, single, careful step at a time.

I

In the airless, dank cellar in the Yellowthread Street police station, Hong Bay, there was a man doing a fair imitation of a dodo.

Dodos didn't cry. There was the faintest glint of moisture in Detective Senior Inspector O'Yee's eyes. It wasn't a fair imitation of a dodo. Wiping away a tear, O'Yee said, 'He's done this to me on purpose!' O'Yee said, 'He's done this to me on purpose and he's done it for no other reason than that I'm a kindly, benign, out of touch fossil in this cruel unthinking world and he's the prime motivating force behind all the cruelty and lack of thought I have to suffer because I am so kindly and bloody benign!' The dodo was wallowing in a mire of self pity. (It was what had killed the dodo off in the first place.) O'Yee said, 'Somewhere, somewhere in the great plan of things there must be some reason, some understandable, underlying, explicable reason why everything always happens to me, but I –' O'Yee said suddenly, 'I'm a married man! *I have children!*'

Standing a little behind him, Constable Lim looked embarrassed. Lim was fresh out of the police training school, and, still, for some unaccountable reason, believed in the basic goodness of people. Lim said, 'With respect, sir, I think Detective Inspector Auden was only –'

The name was like an arrow into the dodo's heart. O'Yee said, 'Arrghh!'

7

'– I believe he was only trying to instruct me in –'

There was a strange glint in O'Yee's eyes. Lim had missed the Tell-Tale Signs Of The Psychopath lecture at the training school due to illness and he failed to recognize it. Lim said, 'I just mentioned to him during the night, sir, that I'd signed for a consignment of evidence and I –' Lim said, 'Senior Constable Sun wasn't around, sir – so I asked Mr Auden – I just asked him to tell me if I'd signed on the right line.' He ventured a nervous smile.

O'Yee said in a strange tone of voice (the voice was from lecture two in the Psychopath Series, also missed), 'The evidence was from Special Branch.'

'Yes, sir.'

O'Yee closed his eyes. O'Yee said with his eyes still closed, 'Please don't say "yes, sir" in that happy, open tone when you talk about Special Branch.' He was trying to be calm. He was failing. O'Yee said, 'Lim, please, for the sake of your future, when you talk about Special Branch stand with your back to the wall and wince!' O'Yee said in a strange burping voice, 'You don't ask Auden if you've signed on the right line with Special Branch.' He winced. 'What you do when you sign for something from Special Branch is just make sure that –' O'Yee asked in sudden alarm, 'Ink? Did you sign in ink?'

He hadn't missed that lecture. Lim said, 'Yes, sir!'

'Wrong! With Special Branch you sign in blood!' O'Yee, staring down at the floor of the long, brick dusty room, said, 'Forty-seven seized handguns and assorted automatic weapons: you actually went up to bloody Auden and told him that you'd signed for forty-seven seized handguns and automatic weapons – from *Special Branch*?' O'Yee, still wincing, said, 'Do you realize that's like telling Jack the Ripper that you've just signed for forty-seven bloody Victorian streetwalkers and a *knife*?' O'Yee said, 'Do you realize that that's like telling –'

Lim said, 'Mr Auden carries a .357 magnum, sir, just like Dirty Harry –'

O'Yee needed a cigarette. He got one out of his packet, but his fingers, with a life of their own, crushed and shredded it

8

into weed before he got it into his mouth. He tried again. His fingers turned the cigarette into pulp. O'Yee said quietly, 'Dirty Harry carries a forty-four magnum!' O'Yee said in a quiet, sad voice, 'I thought it would be bad, but it's even worse than I could have imagined.'

'Sir, couldn't we get Mr Auden back to —'

'No, we couldn't get Mr Auden back again!' O'Yee, starting to hop, said, 'No! Mr Auden is being punished.' Another glint came to his eyes. You didn't need to have attended the lecture on Psychopaths for that one. O'Yee said, 'Mr Auden is being made to suffer and Mr Auden is not coming anywhere near this station until his suffering is complete!' He smiled. Lim stepped back. O'Yee said, 'I don't blame you because you're young and stupid and fresh out of training school.'

'Thank you, sir.'

O'Yee said, 'Hmm.' O'Yee was going quiet. That was a bad sign. O'Yee said, 'I'm a married man.' And reflective: even worse. 'I have children. My children think their Daddy —' Did he brush away a tear? Lim tensed. O'Yee said, 'They think their Daddy is a kindly man.' O'Yee said, 'And he is! What the hell does my children's father know about bloody guns and assorted automatic weapons? I'm a man of peace!' He thought of Auden suffering and said, 'Hahgh! What in God's name possessed you to stand here bloody grinning while Auden took apart forty-seven handguns and assorted bloody automatic weapons the property of *Special Branch*?' O'Yee said, 'It isn't a conspiracy, is it? I mean, it isn't some sort of little plan you and Auden have hatched up between you to —' The eyes narrowed, 'You didn't know Auden *before*, did you?'

'No, sir!' Lim said, 'Couldn't we just ring Special Branch or —'

'Ring up *Special Branch*? It's part of Special Branch's biggest operation for years to cut down on the number of illegal weapons in the Colony!'

'— or Ballistics or the police Armoury or —'

O'Yee said in horror, 'Ring up . . . *Special Branch*?'

'Or Mr Auden, or — or —'

O'Yee said, 'Forty-seven, plus one, two, three, four . . . seven, nine, times, well, on average, twenty-six, times fifty-six plus or minus . . .'

'Sir, I assumed that anyone who carried a – a –' Lim said with a desperate need to impress, 'Sir, it was a Colt Python! I saw a picture of one in a book. That's what Mr Auden carries! A –' Lim said, 'Naturally, sir, I assumed that anyone who carried a Colt Python could strip forty-seven handguns and assorted automatic weapons before breakfast and then, with one hand tied behind his back –!' – That was a nice thought. How about both? And a blindfold and a handy wall and say, a Mexican firing-squad or – O'Yee savoured the thought.

Lim said, 'Sir, naturally I assumed *he could put them all back together again!*' Lim said, 'Sir, Mr O'Yee –'

Ha-ha, ho-ho . . . oh God . . . one thousand six hundred and fifty-six bits of gun all spread out on the floor. Not even spread – O'Yee felt his eyes mist over. *Scattered.* O'Yee, sniffing, said, 'Call me Christopher.'

'Sir –' Lim's eyes also brimmed. Lim said, 'Honest, I'm really, honestly . . .'

The dodo, its head sinking slowly and pathetically onto its shoulders as it saw the approach of evolution and the onset of extinction, made a sniffing noise.

Lim said, 'Christopher . . .' He could see the poor old chap was thinking about his children. Lim said, 'Sir –?'

Lim said . . . His composure broke. Dodoism was on the increase. Lim said in sudden, hopeless, communicated desperation, '*Sir, what the hell are we going to do?*'

9.17 a.m. In his fourth-floor apartment on Beach Road The Far Away Man felt his arm stiffen. He touched it to his mouth and his wrist came away with a smear of blood on it. His mouth was dry and hurting.

On his knees he worked at the catch of his pistol with stiffening hands, pulling back on the barrel latch to open it.

The gun was a silver plated .38 Smith and Wesson target pistol model 1891 with hard rubber grips.

The Far Away Man broke open the barrel and flipped out the fired case and saw it fall like a tiny brass marker onto the thick pile carpet by his leg and lie still.

The Far Away Man drew a long, deep breath.

From a box on the coffee table in front of him, he took another round and slipped it into the breech.

His mouth and arms were hurting.

The Far Away Man closed the gun with difficulty and began to go out again.

It was 9.19.

The Far Away Man drew a long, deep breath.

In Wyang Street, the Government Medical Officer, Doctor Macarthur, said with undisguised delight, 'I can actually see the bullet!' He had an acrid French cigarette going and he let two sudden plumes of smoke out of his nostrils like a satyr having fun. With the black government ambulance parked up against Mr Mui's doorway, he had the scene closed to the street and, his privacy assured, set to scraping bone and brain off the doorway's wide display window and wiping it into a little plastic forensic bag.

He could have been a child spreading jam.

By him, Detective Chief Inspector Harry Feiffer glanced at Mr Mui. Mr Mui was just inside the open door of the shop, doing a sort of involuntary shuffle from side to side. Macarthur moved the shoe shine man's head a little to get at some more mortal paste and the shoe shine man's eyes looked upwards at the door jamb through glazed over waxy eyes and looked straight past Mr Mui to the ceiling of the shop.

Macarthur moved the head again and the eyes came around on a broken ball and socket joint and looked at Mr Mui. The shoe shine man was still sitting on his little wooden shoebox. Macarthur swivelled him around slightly and his arm fell down pointing at a tin of brown shoe polish. He seemed to be disappointed Mr Mui was not going to ask him for a shine. Mr Mui made a hissing sound.

Feiffer said quietly, 'You don't have to watch this.' He looked hard at Mr Mui's face for signs of emotion.

There was no sign of emotion on Mr Mui's face. Mr Mui said, not to Feiffer, but to Macarthur, 'When you deal with death it must give you a satisfied feeling to be still alive.' He was not talking to Macarthur. His eyes travelled to Feiffer.

Macarthur said, 'I've never really thought about it.' He found a sliver of bone mixed in with the grey muck on the window and said, 'Ahh.'

Mr Mui said, 'You know: to look at a clock and see minutes and hours and moments you thought you'd never see. To see –' Mr Mui said curiously, 'It was really quite gentle, not like on TV. There wasn't any kind of –' Mr Mui said, 'I told him it wasn't fair to kill someone like a dog!' He stepped back into the shop and slapped his hands against his thighs as if there was something there, an insect, scrabbling at him with long, sharp legs. Mr Mui said, 'I told him!'

Feiffer got his hand onto Mr Mui's shoulder. It was the shoulder of a soft, ageing man. Under it, in the muscles, there was the lean centre of a young man trying to escape: Feiffer felt the nerves and muscles flickering and twisting for strength. Feiffer said, 'It's all right. You're alive.'

Mr Mui said, 'He wasn't! He wasn't human! He just – he just stood there looking at me through – his eyes looked dead. They looked like a photograph of eyes! I talked and talked to him and the eyes didn't change!' Mr Mui said, 'My ulcer was – I had to piss!' He was making gasping noises, going fast. 'But he didn't! He didn't have to piss and he didn't have any pain! He wasn't even there. He was somewhere else!' Mr Mui shook his head. 'I don't even know who the shoe shine man was. He set up here every day until I opened. It was an arrangement we had. He never made a mess and it got customers looking in the window of my shop while I was closed so I –' Mr Mui said, 'I don't even know his name.'

Feiffer had the shoe shine man's hawker's licence in his hand. Feiffer said, 'His name was Shen.'

'Did he live anywhere?'

'Where he could.' The card had a section on it marked, 'Abode.' The issuing officer had written in English and Cantonese, 'No fixed address.' Feiffer said, 'Nobody saw anything except you.'

'All I saw –' Mr Mui said, 'He just shot him!' It was becoming real. The paste on the side window of his shop was not paste, it was brains. Mr Mui said, 'He just went up next to him and put his hand on his shoulder and he was dead!'

'Did he say anything?'

'Only what I told you. I said– I asked him –' Mr Mui said suddenly, 'I wasn't talking to him or appealing to him or reasoning with him! He was like the weather or –' Mr Mui said, 'Or – or death! I wasn't talking to him! What I was doing was praying to him, I said, "don't you have a doubt" or "a single doubt" or – or something and he –'

'In English?'

'Of course in English! He'd hardly speak Cantonese, would he!'

'Why not?'

'Because he –'

'Because he was a tourist?' Feiffer said, 'Was he dressed like a tourist?'

'No, he –' Mr Mui said, 'No, he –' He put his hands into fists and shook them like a child trying to get his own way. Mr Mui said, 'I just assumed he – all he said to me was "No." No, he didn't have any doubts, no, he –' Mr Mui said, 'You have no idea what he looked like!'

In the doorway there was a grating sound as Macarthur did something with the shoe shine man's neck. Feiffer said quickly, 'No, I don't, but you do.'

'*He looked like death!*'

'Local or imported?'

'It isn't funny!'

'According to you he didn't say anything. You did all the talking.'

'Well, naturally I spoke to him in English because –'

'Because of what?'

13

'Well, because –' Mr Mui said, 'Well, with fair hair and blue eyes he was hardly Chinese, was he?'

'Your sign from the Hong Kong Tourist Office says you also speak German and Spanish.'

'Well, he –' Mr Mui said, 'Well, I –' Mr Mui said – Mr Mui said quietly, 'He was an English-speaking local. He was wearing an expensive locally made grey suit. Not the type tailors make overnight for tourists, but a proper, good quality one that you order from an expensive establishment and wait a month for.'

Feiffer said, 'Yes?' He waited.

Mr Mui said, 'And he was suntanned. Not the way, say the English are when they've lain around a swimming-pool in the Colony for a few days: lightly and a sort of too deep brown, and not the way Australians are – burned down to the bone, but the way –' He looked at Feiffer, 'The way you are, over years here.' Mr Mui said, 'He was a local European resident, about five foot eleven tall, with fair hair and very pale blue eyes.'

'Could he have been wearing contact lenses?'

'You make him sound real!'

Feiffer said, 'Age?'

'I don't know.' Mr Mui said, 'You know Chinese can't tell the age of Europeans any more than Europeans can tell –' The world seemed to be returning to normal. Mr Mui said with what he thought was an encouraging grin, 'How old do you think I am?' He touched at his balding head.

Feiffer said, 'About fifty-five.'

'I'm fifty-four.' Mr Mui said, 'I don't know! He was forty or forty-five! I don't know!'

In the doorway, Macarthur and two policemen were lifting the shoe shine man into the back of the ambulance. There was a sound like mud falling. The mud was grey and it came from the shoe shine man's head. Feiffer said quickly, 'He wasn't death or a ghost or some sort of nemesis, he was real.' He took Mui by the shoulder and turned him away from the view of the doorway to face him, 'What sort of gun was it?'

14

Mr Mui shook his head.

'Was it a pistol or a –'

'It was a pistol.'

'Long barrelled or –'

Mr Mui said, 'I don't know. I don't know anything about –'

'Longer than the sort you see police constables wearing in their holsters or –'

'Longer. It was –' Mr Mui said, 'It looked like one of the guns you see in Westerns, but it – when he lifted it up a little there wasn't that round thing that holds the bullets, the –'

Feiffer said, 'Cylinder.' He gave Mui an encouraging nod, 'A single-shot target pistol or –'

Mui said, 'It was silver plated –' He looked out to the doorway where one of the ambulancemen was inside the ambulance struggling to pull the body inside. Mr Mui said, 'After – after you've prayed to a statue or an idol or something you forget whether your prayers were answered or not and all you remember is the picture in your mind of the idol . . .'

'You're doing just fine.' Mr Mui's eyes were on the shoe shine man's feet as they went into the ambulance. The ankles went limp. Feiffer, moving to block his view, touched him again on the shoulder. 'Did you notice anything about his hands or his neck or –?'

Mr Mui said, 'His eyes. They weren't there.' He shook his head, 'They were there, but they weren't –' He remembered a question. 'No, he wasn't wearing contact lenses. His eyes were dull – they were –' He searched for the word, 'They were *empty*.' Mr Mui said suddenly, 'And when he walked he looked tired: he –' Mr Mui shook his head. Had it all been real? 'He seemed –'

'What?'

'*Heavy*. He –' Mr Mui said, 'And the way he stood. He was a thin man but he seemed planted on the ground like –' Mr Mui said, 'He looked tired.' He grimaced hard at Feiffer to make him understand, 'It was as if something had drained out of his eyes and he was –' Mr Mui said, 'He was –'

In the doorway the ambulance doors closed with a bang.

Mr Mui shook his head. 'He was –' He looked at Feiffer's face. The hair, like The Far Away Man's was fair, bleached by years of sun, and the eyes, blue, but deeper, different, and the colour of the skin: darker, somehow, again, deeper, and the way he held his head, and the mouth – Mr Mui said quietly and without doubt, 'It was a long gun. It was heavy in his hand.' Mr Mui said, 'He wasn't there to rob me. He was waiting. I didn't talk him out of anything. He was just waiting.' Mr Mui said, 'All the things I said to him were –'

He wondered what to do about his daughter.

'All the things I said to him were rubbish! They didn't matter! He was waiting. I don't know for what. Maybe for the shoe shine man, but not for me.' He looked out at the waiting ambulance and found he could see the black painted body without seeing what was inside. Mr Mui said gasping, 'Clocks and minutes and hours and all the things that go on after you're not there anymore . . .' Mr Mui said, 'I thought I should be grateful to him, sparing me, but now –' He thought of the pale eyes looking at him. Mr Mui said fiercely, 'He wasn't here for me at all!'

Mr Mui said without doubt, 'He was bleeding from the mouth all the time he was here.' He thought for a moment of his daughter. Mr Mui said, 'He wasn't here for me at all! My life goes on! It's going to go on for years!' He took Feiffer by the shoulder and almost shook him to share his exultation. Mr Mui said, 'He was bleeding from the mouth all the time he was here!' Mr Mui, released, said triumphantly, 'His eyes and his walk and his – and his –' Mr Mui said, 'I know what he was and I know why he looked the way he did!' He let go of Feiffer and beat his fists down onto his thighs again and again.

Mr Mui said in utter, saved joy, 'He was bleeding from the mouth all the time he was here! Your European, your English-speaking local, your five-foot-eleven, fair-haired, suntanned, pale-eyed killer of shoe shine men, I know what he was! What he was –' Mr Mui looked around his shop, 'What he was –' He couldn't believe it. He was safe. Life was – Life was –

16

Mr Mui said exultantly, '*What he was was a dying man! And he hadn't come for me at all!*'

Mr Mui said with a bitter look on his face, 'And my daughter and her new husband, as far as I'm concerned, can go straight, directly, by the fastest available route, right to fucking *Hell*!'

Jade possesses the five major virtues which man should strive for. By its warmth and bright lustre it typifies charity. Because of its translucence it reveals its inner faults and typifies sincerity.

When struck, it sends out a note which is pure and so typifies wisdom. Jade can be broken but never bent; thus it typifies courage.

Though it might have sharp edges it will not harm; thus it typifies . . .

Mr Mui's shop was full of jade, but as he looked around he failed to see any of it.

Instead, as he had always done, he saw only objects.

9.47 a.m.

In the ambulance, Doctor Macarthur found something in the shoe shine man's pocket. It was a wad of carefully folded yellow paper, two separate pages.

There was printing on the pages and the faint impression of two rubber stamps, one on each page, and two names, again, one on each page:

– OR REVACCINATION AGAINST CHOLERA
  DE REVACCINATION CONTRA LE CHOLÉRA

Macarthur pursed his lips curiously and looked at the two written-in names on the yellow pages.

They meant nothing to him and he put them to one side and looked again with interest at the awful, killing wound in the shoe shine man's head in case he had missed something.

9.47 a.m.

In Icehouse Street The Far Away Man, dabbing at his mouth with his handkerchief, began walking south.

2

The reassuring thing about the home video and electronics revolution was that when the revolution came you probably wouldn't be able to hear it for the noise.

In Kamikaze Mansions on Hong Bay Road near the waterfront, Detective Inspector Phil Auden, disassembler of guns, sufferer of O'Yee's wrath, and possessor of what were fast becoming the most abused ears east of Suez, shouted at a hopelessly inadequate volume, 'I can't hear a thing for Chinese bloody opera and bloody early morning radio!'

Kamikaze Mansions was a giant fourteen-storey apartment house built in the shape of a U. He and Detective Inspector Spencer were standing in the centre concourse at ground level looking up. The noise from four hundred and ninety apartments filled with televisions, stereos, radios, record-players and Japanese home organs was coming straight down. Spencer, cupping his hand to his ear, said, 'What?' A posse of white-coated men with push carts and wheeled trolleys selling sugar cane drinks, hot meals, blancmange dishes and soy bean drinks went trundling, creaking, bell ringing and shouting by on their way to the fourteen floors. The lifts that took them up went ding, crash, wheeze. Somewhere someone with a predilection for collecting sound recordings of the space shuttle warming up went click – whoom! and, someone else, bored at the quiet, let fly with a few high notes on his home trumpet course. Spencer shouted, 'I can't hear a word you're saying!'

Auden shouted, 'Doesn't anybody in this place go to *work*?' He moved to another spot on the concourse to be blasted by noise that sounded like a cross between Wagner and a cat being gutted coming straight down. Auden shrieked, 'This is all bloody O'Yee's idea!' He saw Spencer mouth something about 'you shouldn't have' and then caught the mouth shape for 'gun'. Auden yelled back, hopping and waddling as his head vibrated between Wagner and the cat, 'I just wanted to make sure they were all intact! I was doing O'Yee a favour! I was saving him the trouble of –' He mouthed a further stream of explanations, but the cat-gutting took them all away. Auden yelled, 'This is a job for Uniformed, not us!' Three electric guitarists on the ground floor decided to have a race to see who could finish the scales first. No one won. Auden yelled, 'How the hell can we hear anyone kill themselves in this bloody racket?'

The trumpeter let fly a few high Cs.

One of the trolleys on the second floor began a rendition of *Greensleeves* on what sounded like the full campanological complement of the belfry – including Quasimodo – of Notre-Dame cathedral.

The home organs organized. They all went off together.

The Cantonese versions of *Driller Killer* and *The Acoustic Murderer* were the home top-volume videos of the week.

Auden yelled, 'God Almighty!'

Somewhere, there must have been someone who wasn't plugged into the twentieth century.

There was. On the third floor there was a man building a boat with a petrol driven chainsaw.

Auden yelled, 'He's punishing me, that's what he's doing!' He ducked as a blast of noise that could have been someone doing lesson three of the Home Jackhammer Course enveloped him. 'He's punishing me because I tried to help and check the bloody guns for him before –' The Jackhammer Man had a brother taking Swiss Yodelling For Foreigners, Auden shrieked, 'I was just doing it as a favour – as a surprise!' Auden, still vibrating, appealed to the heavens, 'How the hell was I supposed to know I couldn't put them all back together again?' He stopped shouting. He said, '*God Almighty* –!'

High up in the maelstrom of noise, rising straight above it, there was a terrible gut-twisting shriek as, for the fourteenth time in six days, some poor lost soul hurled himself into oblivion straight down at least twelve or thirteen solidly packed floors of high-rise humanity.

There was an echoing *thump!* as his flying body struck the cement.

There was the long, sad echo of his cry as the wind took it and –

There was the slow, rolling reverberation of the ground as the Earth itself –

There was –

There was nothing.

The invisible suicide of Kamikaze Mansions had done it again.

For a moment all the noise stopped.

Auden looked at Spencer.

Spencer, glancing around the concourse, shook his head.

The echo of High-Dive Henry's death-shriek wafted with declining volume through the corridors and verandas on all the fourteen storeys of the apartment block as the apartment block dwellers waited.

Sepulchral silence.

There was not a single dead body anywhere on the cement concourse. Auden said quietly to Spencer, 'Bill?'

Spencer shook his head.

There was nothing. Spencer said, 'I don't know . . .' He looked around the concourse for the second time and for the second time – Spencer said, 'I heard him. I heard him fall. I heard the thump.' He scratched his head and looked around for the third time. Spencer said, 'I actually felt the vibration.' He looked up at the apartments.

The apartment block was silent.

Auden said –

Spencer said –

They were all waiting. They saw faces peeping out through curtains, watching.

Spencer said –

There was another terrible shriek and High-Dive Henry came down again.

There was a terrible 'thump!' as his body hit the concourse.

There was a terrible vacancy on the concourse where his body had hit and where his body had hit there was no body.

Spencer said –

Auden said –

Whatever he said was lost instantly as, in all the apartments of Kamikaze Mansions on Hong Bay Road, four hundred and ninety fingers went for the volume buttons simultaneously and, in a welter of mind-numbing chaos, almost blew him completely off his feet with the noise.

How difficult was it to put a gun back together after some idiot had taken it apart?

It wasn't difficult. It was easy. After all, when you came down to it, what was a pistol – a firearm – but a piece of pipe with a hole at both ends and something connected to give the cap a good whack to get the bullet off in the direction of he you wanted bulleted?

Simplicity itself. It was simply one shuffling step further along the line of progress from the bludgeon. No, it *was* a bludgeon: the only difference was that instead of having the bludge stuck on the end of a piece of tree branch the bludge was stuck on the end of the cartridge and the bludgeation took place, not at messy tree-branch length, but at pipe range where it was a little cleaner and more out of sight. It was simplicity itself, pathetic.

O'Yee sighed. How little Man had progressed in the last few million years. Well, at least it meant there would always be work for policemen. Holding the first weapon in his hand and offering it to Lim like a shallowly incised decorated bone from Man's first campsite, O'Yee said sadly, 'What is this atavistic object but a piece of roughly forged ore and a simple mechanism to give it motion?'

Lim said, 'Yes, sir.' He looked at the gun and wondered how he could ever have been so callow as to think that merely because a man carried a .357 magnum— Lim said, 'Sir, it is nothing more than a totem object to bring a false sense of power to man's poor, pathetic struggles against the incomprehensibility of natural forces.' He nodded. He looked at O'Yee.

Lim's English was impeccable. O'Yee could not have put it better himself.

Lim said, 'A contemptible, shoddy attempt by an awkward fool to create out of a few found objects a third-rate tool for an ignoramus bent on nothing more than the cowardly and pathetic attempt to destroy his fellow-man.' Lim said with a sneer, 'Garbage. Hardly worthy of our time; the outward physical manifestation of a brutish mind unknowing of the joys of the act of original creation or fine, humanitarian selflessness.' They had never told him at training school that police work could be so literate. Lim, shaking his head in gentle disappointment, gazed at the proffered weapon and went, 'Tch, tch, tch.'

O'Yee, nodding, went, 'Hmm, hmm, hmm . . .'

In his hand, O'Yee patted the rubber-band-powered, copper-pipe barrelled zip gun and, with a snap, put back the bolt from the window latch on top that the maker had nailed on to fire the cartridge. O'Yee, with a flourish, said easily, 'Thus I reassemble it.'

Lim said, 'Gosh!'

O'Yee said, 'Hmm, hmm, hmm.'

Only forty-six revolvers and pistols plus assorted automatic weapons to go.

Colts.

Webleys.

Mausers.

Lugers.

Assorted automatic weapons.

One thousand six hundred and fifty-six bits.

Lim said, 'Wow!'

O'Yee said, 'Huh!'

O'Yee said in sudden panic, 'Lim, are you sure all these bits only came out of forty-seven guns and assorted automatic weapons?'

They had. The floor was covered in them: all shapes and sizes, springs, screws, receivers, barrels, breeches, sears, hammers, butts, bodies and bolts, things that looked like chambers – guns.

How little Man had progressed. O'Yee, getting down on his knees in a sudden panic at the incomprehensible natural forces surrounding him, tensing his shoulders, gathered an armful of objects around his campfire at night and from somewhere, hearing a dinosaur roar as it spied a meandering, doomed dodo, did what any Modern Man would have done in the same circumstances:

O'Yee said, '*Aarghh!*'

10.21 a.m. In Icehouse Street, The Far Away Man entered a little park opposite The Windjammer Club and sat down. All his joints were aching and he had to adjust his legs two or three times to find relief. He touched at his mouth with his handkerchief.

Across the street people were going into The Windjammer Club for morning coffee or a drink: old men in civilian clothes and younger ones in the uniform of the Navy or the Merchant Marine.

The Far Away Man rested his hand lightly against the bulge the gun in his belt made against his coat and watched them.

There were children playing in the park, their thoughts full of activity and life.

The Far Away Man's thoughts were full of nothing but decay and death.

He felt a spot of warm blood at the corner of his mouth.

He touched at it with his handkerchief and waited.

* * *

– OR REVACCINATION AGAINST *CHOLERA*.
– DE REVACCINATION CONTRE LE *CHOLÉRA*

> This is to certify that
> Je soussigné(e) que
> date of birth
> né(e) le
> sex
> sexe
> whose signature follows
> dont la signature suit

has on the date indicated been vaccinated or revaccinated against

> CHOLERA

a été vacciné(e) ou revacciné(e) contre le CHOLÉRA à la date indiquée.

The names, both written in the same firm hand in ink, read, *U Ne*, born *8.1.1947*, sex *Male*, and *Koo Teh-cheung*, born *6.7.1951*, sex also *Male*.

In the morgue, Feiffer turned the two identical sheets of yellow paper over in his hand.

The reverses of the pages contained only printed spaces for further lists of inoculations and the names and stamps of the doctors who gave them.

The spaces were blank.

INTERNATIONAL CERTIFICATION OF VACCINA-TION. The pages had been torn out from a double spread in the certificate book, and where the stamps of the issuing authorities would have been on the verso there was only the faintest arc of blue ink and a few letters that probably formed part of the word HEALTH. That narrowed the issuing authority down from every country in the world to only those which had English as either its first, its official, or its second language.

The name U Ne narrowed it down to about twenty million male Burmese or people of Burmese extraction, and Koo Teh-cheung, certainly to no more than about one billion Chinese.

By the stainless steel table in the centre of the government mortuary Feiffer put the two pages carefully in the centre of his notebook and signed a receipt for them in the Dead On Arrival book by the shoe shine man's feet.

At the end of the table, the shoe shine man's broken leather sandals were on top of the tied bundle of his clothes. Feiffer took one of them up and turned it over. It was of cheap quality and worn down from much walking. He looked at the shoe shine man's feet and saw callouses and corns on the waxy skin and, on the right foot, the tell-tale twisting of the toes that signalled the onset of a crippling arthritis.

The shoe shine man lay naked on the steel table, his head moving slightly from time to time on its little wooden retaining frame as Macarthur worked away inside it with long stainless steel forceps.

There was a click and Macarthur, for once not smoking, said, 'Got it.' It was the bullet. 'It blew out the side of his head without passing through.' Macarthur, leaning down with his eyes against the exit wound like a man peering down a tunnel, said, 'Instantaneous. It's taken away half of his brain.' He looked down at the plastic bag by the shoe shine man's waxen arm, 'I think I got it all from the window.' He looked up, 'I can weigh it if you like, but it means taking the rest of the brain out.' Macarthur said, 'I'm no gun expert, but it looks like a thirty-eight to me.' He popped the bullet into yet another plastic bag and handed it over to Feiffer for labelling. Macarthur, glancing for the first time at the shoe shine man's face, asked with only mild curiosity, 'Was he anybody?'

Feiffer shook his head. 'Shen. Age forty-one, born Hong Kong, three minor convictions for obstruction or hawking without a licence, no fixed address.' Feiffer glanced at the feet again, 'He was what he appears to be: a shoe shine man.' He glanced down at the open DOA book. 'Contents of pockets, six dollars and eighty cents, one out of date fifty-cent betting slip, one book of matches and three cigarettes and two pages from two International Vaccination Certificates.' He shrugged, 'Carefully folded and carried in the top pocket of his shirt.'

The shoe shine man's head was askew on the wooden block with its eyes open. The eyes stared dully at Feiffer on the spot where he stood and, as he moved to shut the DOA book, went on staring at where he had been. Feiffer said, 'From what Mui told me the man who did it was a European, probably a local resident, probably English-speaking – Mui claims he said, "No" at one stage – about five eleven or six foot tall, forty to forty-five years old, thin, fair haired, blue eyes and dying.' He moved nearer the shoe shine man's open head, saw what Macarthur had been seeing, and moved away.

Macarthur said, 'Oh? What of?'

'He was bleeding from the mouth.' Feiffer looked down at the shoe shine man's face still watching the empty spot and closed the eyelids with his fingertips. The head, moved fractionally, rolled against its still relaxed muscles and came down onto the chest in an attitude of prayer. Feiffer said, 'What could that be?'

'Could be anything.' Macarthur, not caring for his work being disturbed, went back and moved the shoe shine man's head back to its original position. His hand was on the exit wound. Something grey dribbled out through his fingers. Macarthur said, 'It could be just a cut lip.' He shrugged. The living did not interest him greatly. 'It takes quite a lot to actually kill someone, you know, Harry. It isn't like television where you can just tap your head against the leg of a table and expire. It takes quite a lot of effort to actually get yourself really certifiably deceased.' He patted the shoe shine man's head in appreciation of the trouble the shoe shine man had taken to get himself really, certifiably deceased. 'For a dying man, the whoever that did this was steady enough.' He couldn't keep his hands off the wound, 'This is right through the left temple transversely through the brain out behind the right ear.' He looked up. 'Anything else I can do for you? I can do a full open body post mortem if you want to see what he would have died from if he hadn't died from this. But I can tell you now if you really want to know.' He looked down at the wound and actually put his fingers in, 'I can feel it. He would

26

have died of a brain tumour in a couple of years.' He looked happy. He said, 'I saw it in his eyes the first time I examined him.'

'Well done.'

Macarthur said, 'Thank you very much.' He looked for a moment as if he was even considering dealing with live people one of these days. He lit a French cigarette, smelled and looked suddenly Satanic, and the look was back under control. In that awful room, Macarthur, with a cheering grin, said quietly to the shoe shine man, 'Well, he would have died anyway. At least this way it was quick.'

Feiffer said, 'Yeah.' Under the closed eyelids the shoe shine man's eyes went on staring. His feet were calloused and twisted from walking. In his pockets, apart from two folded pages from other people's inoculation certificates and three cigarettes, he had had exactly six dollars and eighty cents.

Feiffer said quietly, 'Yeah. It makes you wonder why he didn't just cut his own throat at birth and have done with it.'

The shoe shine man lay still and forever dead on the stainless-steel tray, everything he had ever been or might have wanted to be smashed out of him in a single obliterating flash of power and light and, in that awful, dead, tiled place, try as he could, Feiffer could not think of a single reason why it should have happened.

It was 11.03 a.m. and, in the park in Icehouse Street, as the civilians and men in uniform went into The Windjammer Club for their coffee or first drink of the morning, the children in the park decided to play somewhere else and left The Far Away Man to himself.

He did not notice them go.

With infinite patience, The Far Away Man waited.

3

The two yellow pages from the vaccination documents had to mean something. In the Detectives' Room, Feiffer put down the telephone on his desk and said, 'Nothing! I've been on to everyone from Criminal Records to the tax office to the anti-secret-society squad, and what the two names on the pages mean is nothing, and what Shen was was a shoe shine man.' He looked down at the glistening layer of moisture on his desk. The overhead fan seemed to have gone on work-to-rule and the heat coming in through the open window was coating everything in the room with a layer of glistening moisture, 'I've even looked in the telephone directory and the electoral roll just in case he was one of the local millionaires with a sexual fetish for cleaning shoes before he started business on his yacht.' He wiped his hand across the desk and his hand came away wet. 'But he wasn't. He was a shoe shine man.'

'Of no fixed address.' O'Yee's desk was also awash with condensation. He took his glasses off and wiped at his eyes.

'Of no fixed address and of no witnesses.' Feiffer said, 'And now he's dead.' It was unbelievable. Feiffer said, 'According to Mui, this – this – this far away man came to his shop a little after eight and just stood there for more than forty minutes, not saying anything, not evidently taking any notice of any-thing, not – and then, suddenly, calmly – according to Mui, almost tranquilly – wanders out of the shop and puts a bullet in the temple of a man shining shoes in the bloody doorway!' It was insane. Feifer said, 'No talk, no fuss, just bang! Right in the temple and out behind the ear.' Feiffer said with a total lack of understanding of the mind behind it, 'I once had to shoot a pet dog and I did it with considerably more emotion than that!'

'Could he be a hit man?'

'A what?' Feiffer said, 'A what? A hit man? Have you ever run across a real hit man? I mean, a real one-hundred-percent-do-nothing-else-for-a-living professional killer?'

O'Yee said, 'One or two.'

'So have I and they're not cultured, calm, bloody Greek Stoics like something out of a Frederick Forsyth novel: they're usually half drunk bloody ex-pimps or bar-room bouncers who aren't any good for anything else but pulling a trigger! And, if, in the unlikely event they could even manage it physically, if they stood around in a shop for forty minutes they wouldn't have stayed there in silence, they'd have spilled out their entire sad life stories to someone like Mui, begged his understanding and the name of the nearest good lawyer and then tried to borrow the price of a drink off him!' Feiffer said, 'And they don't kill shoe shine men.' There was something ungraspably evil about someone waiting in silence to kill. Feiffer said, 'Mui said he didn't even sweat.' He made a derisive sound at the back of his throat, 'Mui said he thought he was the original victim, but he talked him out of it.' Feiffer said, 'I think all Mui did was just talk.'

'What about the gun?'

'Nothing. Sands at Ballistics says from a quick examination that the bullet's an old-style thirty-eight with heavy lubricating cannelures probably fired from some sort of pistol made around the turn of the century. Mui says it was a single-shot target pistol, silver plated.' Feiffer said before O'Yee could comment, 'And professional hit men don't use single-shot pistols. In my experience, they either use a sawed-off double-barrelled twelve-gauge if they can get it, and, if they can't, a piece of gas pipe loaded with gunpowder and a one-inch

29

ballbearing.' Feiffer said irritably, more to himself than O'Yee, 'No, he wasn't any sort of hit man.'

'Then what was he?'

'I don't know!' The heat in the room was getting to him. Feiffer said, 'I should be out on the street doing something, not sitting here speculating, but the simple fact of the matter is that I haven't got the faintest idea what street to do anything on!' He looked down at the two yellow pages. They meant nothing. They had to mean something. Feiffer said quietly, 'All that poor bastard in the morgue had on him was a total of six dollars and eighty cents!'

O'Yee said nothing.

'And these.' Feiffer touched at one of the yellow pages and lifted it between the fingernails of his thumb and index finger. Feiffer said irritably, 'You don't even need them anymore. Smallpox has been eradicated, and as for cholera – U Ne and Koo Teh-cheung: it might as well have been Smith and Brown. According to the bloody Burmese Embassy, U Ne, in Burmese *is* bloody Brown!' He wiped at his face and looked down at his hand. It was shining with sweat. Feiffer said quietly, 'According to Sands, when one of those old-style bullets hits you it's like being smashed in the face by an express train. They don't just drill a hole through you, they literally take half your head away.'

O'Yee said quietly, 'Harry –' O'Yee said, 'Look, it happens. Unless you get lucky and some bright cop picks up your man from the description for illegal parking or jaywalking or something –'

'How is he supposed to do that? Have you read the description? It fits half the Europeans in the Colony!' Feiffer said with sudden force, 'Mui, the great talker, couldn't even work out how old the man was till I pushed him to it! Have you seen the description? It says "age: about forty-five – question-mark – about six feet tall, blue eyed and fair haired – question-mark". It could fit half the Swedish Embassy, it could fit Bill Spencer.' Feiffer said, 'It could fit me!' He got his handkerchief out to wipe the moisture from his hands, but the handkerchief was also wet. Feiffer said, 'Oh, the answer's simple: we just mobilize every copper from here to bloody Timbuctoo and we arrest everybody, starting at tall bloody seventeen-year-old adolescents on college vacation from the bright-toothed, corn-fed prairies to bloody Thor Heyerdahl as he floats by on his raft, and we say, "Pardon me, shot any good shoe shine men lately?" '

O'Yee said warily, 'It's the heat. You're letting it get to you.' O'Yee said, 'He's a psycho. It could have been anybody he shot.'

'Then why didn't he shoot Mui?' Feiffer asked, 'And where's his pleasure in it? He didn't get any pleasure from it. He just stood there, not listening to Mui, so he got no pleasure from anyone begging; Mui evidently said to him, "Don't you have any doubts", or something like that, and he, evidently, said, "No", so he was reasonably rational; he had a one-round single-shot pistol, loaded, and he intended to use it— And—and he killed Shen with a single shot in the temple that must have wiped him out like a pile-driver, and then he just walked away.' Feiffer demanded, 'Is he a bloody psycho? If he's a psycho, where the hell did he get his satisfaction from killing a bloody *shoe shine man*?'

'He could have picked anybody!'

'He knocked on Mui's door to get him to open! If he'd wanted anybody why the hell didn't he blast Mui out of bloody existence the moment he opened the door?' Feiffer said, 'The whole time he was there was an off time. It's just before office rush hour and just after the time kids walk to school for early classes. All he had to do was knock on the door, stand there for a second talking to Mui until the street was clear and then let him have it. But he didn't. He went inside the shop off the street and stood there with his back to the street so no one passing would see the gun.' Feiffer said, 'The shoe shine man hadn't even set up his box properly. When I saw him the tins of polish were still unopened. The Far Away Man, or whatever Mui calls him, didn't give a damn: he was like bloody Julius Caesar, came, saw, conquered – came in, went out, killed. Bang! End

31

of story.' It wasn't the heat getting to him, it was something else. Feiffer said quietly, 'And, what bothers me is that I think he's going to do it again.'

'For what? *Why?*'

Six dollars and eighty cents, and three cigarettes. In the Morgue, by now, the shoe shine man's tied-up bundle of clothes would be in a locked steel cupboard awaiting claimants. There would be no claimants. The sandals, worn down from much walking, would be on top of the bundle, also awaiting – Six dollars and eighty cents, one out-of-date fifty-cent betting slip, a book of matches and three cigarettes . . .

Feiffer said, 'For these.' He tapped at the two yellow pages with his knuckles. Maybe it was the heat. He could not get the picture of the shoe shine man's eyes out of his mind and the excavation where the right side of the head had been. Feiffer said quietly, 'It has to be. He has to have been killed for these.'

Maybe it was the heat. The shoes, worn down from much walking. Six dollars and eighty cents, a betting slip, matches and three cigarettes . . .

And two yellow pages from two International Health Certificate books . . .

Feiffer said with a strange, certain look in his eyes, 'Because, Christopher, they were all he had . . .'

U Ne; sex: *Male*; date of birth: *8.1.47.*

Koo Teh-cheung; sex: *Male*; date of birth: *6.7.51.*

At 11.18 a.m. with his hands and face glistening with sweat, Feiffer stared down at the two names on the yellow pages and, shaking his head, wondered who the hell they were.

His eyes were going. In the park, The Far Away Man put his hands to his face and pressed.

His eyes were going. Around him, he heard sounds: traffic, people talking, noises, echoes. He heard a car start across the road and then someone selling something shout the nature of his wares, then, as a group of people must have walked close to the edge of the park, a babble of voices and laughter.

His eyes were going. He pressed at the sockets and there was nothing under his hands but blackness. He felt all the joints in his body ache and he pulled his heels up closer to the bench and dug them hard against the grass to give himself purchase.

He felt himself sway.

He heard sounds, voices, people. Across the street people were going into The Windjammer Club for coffee or drinks. He heard —

He felt a sudden sharp pain at the back of his neck and pulled his hands away from his face and thought he cried out.

There was no sound.

He felt warmth at the side of his mouth: blood. Blood was coming out of his mouth in a warm trickle and he tried to rub it away with his palm and felt it smear on his chin.

His sight came back: he saw a swimming blur of grass on the ground in front of him, and then, for a moment, his shoes and then his legs as he brought his legs up and reached down to clasp his knees to steady himself.

A claw crushing him together like a rubber ball being squeezed hit him in the stomach and he thought he cried out.

There was no sound.

Across the street people were going into The Windjammer Club: he saw blurs of movement going up the steps and disappearing into a swimming, black hole. He thought, for a moment, he —

The claw released him and he thought, for a moment, he slept.

Across the street people were going into The Windjammer Club.

The Far Away Man put his hand gently to his face.

There was not a single drop of perspiration on The Far Away Man's hands or face. His skin was smooth and unhuman, like a puppet's.

The Far Away Man's hand touched reassuringly on the bulge the long silver gun in his belt made under his coat.

The pain was gone.

It had receded.

For a moment, The Far Away Man closed his eyes.

In Kamikaze mansions, Auden bent down and touched at the cement of the concourse with the palm of his hand. The cement concourse felt like it had come through earth re-entry with the tape-recorder nut's recording of the space shuttle. It was red hot. His hand came away sizzling. Auden, making szz, szz noises, slapped his hand under his armpit to cool it off. The hand burned through his shirt and curled all the hairs under his armpit. Auden said, even above the residual noise of the music, bells, shrieks, yells and stereos, 'No! Never! It's a crazy idea!'

Spencer had his own gun wrapped up in his coat on the ground next to him and was happily pressing buttons on his calculator. Spencer said, 'Look, think about it logically. There are fourteen floors of apartments, right?' He waited.

Auden's gun had slipped. He reached in under his coat to push it up again and touched the metal cylinder. That was a mistake. Auden said, 'Right, right!' The leather of his holster was melting. He squeezed at it and his mutilated hand came away a brown colour. Auden, gasping, said, 'So?'

'"So" is that the mistake the Uniformed people who tried this made was going to each and every flat' – Spencer went click, click, click on the calculator – 'Thirty-five flats on each floor times fourteen floors, which is –' He held the calculator up to find a bit of shade to see the read-out. 'Which is four hundred and ninety flats, and what did they ask?' Was it four hundred and ninety? That seemed a lot. He twisted the instrument. It was four hundred and ninety. Times say an average of five and a half people per apartment and that was – Spencer said, losing his thread, 'Gosh!'

Auden felt a clang under his coat as one of the buckles on the holster gave way. He reached in to fix it and all of the buckles were OK. It must have been one of his vital organs giving out.

Spencer said, 'And what did they ask? They asked, "Any idea where the strange death shriek is coming from?"' Spencer said, 'In what? In this racket?' He tapped the calculator. 'And what did they manage to find out?' He looked down at the calculator face to make absolutely certain the figure was right. 'They managed to find out – not surprisingly – that as the two thousand six hundred and ninety-five people in the apartments heard the scream starting they all turned up their radios or videos or whatever to drown it out.' He looked up to where the now abated noise was coming from. On the spot, the figure sounded right. 'And what did they get from that? They got a resounding nothing.'

Good. That was what Spencer was going to get too. A resounding nothing. Less. A resounding – His hand, in the sun, was going green. Auden said, 'Look, Bill, be reasonable. The guns were a mistake. Sooner or later O'Yee's going to see that and put me onto something sensible. He doesn't want us to actually solve anything – he just wants to inflict a bit of suffering.' There was another clang under his coat, then a sort of clomph noise. Auden said desperately, 'That's OK, I don't mind! I'm suffering! I'm happy!' Auden said, 'OK?'

'All you have to do is put your ear to the ground the moment we hear the shriek and I'll time it on the stopwatch and then –' He was still clicking. 'And then, because an object falls at thirty-two feet per second all you have to do is put your ear to the ground the moment we hear the shriek. I'll time the interval, and then, the moment you hear the reverberation in the ground when he hits I'll simply divide the elapsed time by the formula and we'll know exactly what floor he fell from.' Spencer said encouragingly, 'It's easy.' Spencer said, 'I did Science at school. It'll work.' He waved his calculator. 'It'll cut it down to one floor, thirty-five apartments and –' He went click, click, click – 'and no more than' – click – 'One hundred and ninety two and a half people. Give or take a few.'

'Why the hell can't we do all this when it's cooler?' Auden looked at his hand. It had gone a sort of puce. 'Like about midnight?'

'Because these people are shift workers. They sub-let their flats on a shift basis. By midnight we wouldn't be dealing with the same people.' He paused. There was a flaw there somewhere. He looked at his calculator.

Auden said, 'Hmm.' He thought of O'Yee.

'It's logical.'

Auden said, 'Hmm.' He waited, but all his internal organs seemed to be still doing what they were supposed to. Auden said, 'Say he jumps from the top floor. How long am I supposed to keep my ear to the ground?'

Click, click, click.

Spencer said, 'Um . . .' He went click, click, click. Spencer said, 'Not long.' He looked up with a grin, 'Or he could jump from the first in which case –' Spencer said, 'Look, you don't actually have to put your ear right to the ground. You can put it a few inches away. Just so long as you hear the thump.'

'I don't need my ear to the ground to hear the thump!' Auden said, 'Why the hell can't I just listen carefully and feel the vibration through my shoes?'

There was a pause.

Spencer said, 'All right.' He looked hurt. Spencer said, 'I'm just trying to help.'

'I appreciate that.'

Spencer said, 'I didn't disassemble the guns.'

Auden looked at his hand.

Spencer said, 'All I was trying to do was give you –'

'All right!'

'You can have the arrest.'

'Thanks.'

Spencer said, 'But if you feel –' He started to put his calculator away.

Auden said, 'All right!'

'I can see your point.' The calculator was brand new. He had just learned how to do integral calculus on it. He looked disappointed. Spencer said –

Auden said, '*All right!*' What was an ear. He had two. Auden said, 'All right, I'll put my ear on the ground, all right!'

The calculator came out again. In the bright sun it was glinting with newness. Spencer said, 'Thanks very much.' Spencer said warmly, 'It's the way the Indians used to do it to hear when the Iron Horse was coming.' He grinned.

Great. Terrific. Wonderful. Auden said, 'Oh.' He leaned

down and touched at the pulsating melting concrete. His hand was numb and there was no pain.

Auden said, 'Sure. Why not? It's worth a try.'

He got down on his knees and, as the magic lines on hunting ground that carried White Man's Iron Horse burned straight through his trousers and melted both knees into liquid blobs of fire, said in happy expectation, 'Oh, oh, oh, oh!'

There he was! Spencer yelled, '*Now!*' High-Dive Henry shrieked, 'Aaarrrgghhhhh!' Auden was down on his knees with his ear to the ground and his eyes bulging as smoke came out of his nostrils. Spencer yelled, 'We're going to get him, Phil!' He had the stopwatch going. It was going click, click, clickety-click . . . Spencer yelled, 'Thirty-two feet a second!' He was counting off the floors in reverse, 'Fourteen . . . thirteen . . . twelve . . .' He looked down at Auden. Auden's hands seemed to have collapsed under him and he was lying full length on the cement with a strange, cooking look on his face, '. . . ten . . . nine . . . eight . . .' Spencer yelled, 'I'm counting in reverse! When he stops all we have to do is subtract the number of floors from the total' – that calculator could do anything – 'And we've got him!' Spencer said, 'Six . . . five . . . four . . .' He looked happy. Spencer said, 'Here it comes . . . three . . . two – he must have jumped from the top floor – one.' He looked triumphant. 'One . . .' He looked strange. '. . . minus one . . . minus two . . . minus three . . . minus four . . .' Spencer said in a small voice, 'Oh, gosh . . . minus six . . . minus seven, minus . . .' He looked at Auden with a sort of grin. Auden looked back with a sort of grimace. 'Minus . . . eight . . .' Spencer said meekly, 'I don't think this is going to work . . .' Spencer said, 'Phil, I think you can get up now.'

According to the calculator High-Dive Henry, so far, had fallen twenty-seven floors from a fourteen-storey building. And he was still falling. Spencer said, 'Phil . . .'

Thump!

Auden mouthed, 'Ah . . .' He raised one gnarled, burned finger. Auden said, 'Ah . . .'

Thump! Thump! Thump!

Auden said, 'Agg . . .' The gnarled, burned finger stayed in mid-air. It seemed a little twisted, like an old stump. Auden said, 'Agg?'

Spencer said, 'Um . . .'

There were – according to the calculator – no less than two thousand six hundred and ninety-five (give or take a few) residents in Kamikaze Mansions. For the last twenty-seven seconds, for the first time in six days of non-stop solid noise, they had been silent.

They too, had all believed totally in pocket calculators.

No more. Jerking back from their pulled-back curtains and crack-opened doors into the safe, dark haven of shriek and thump obliterating mega-decibelity, they all went for their Volume and On buttons with a single shattering, annihilating, all-enveloping blast.

He saw him. He saw Sharwood.

In the park, The Far Away Man's eyes had cleared and there, going up the steps into The Windjammer Club, he saw him.

He saw Sharwood.

The long, silver-plated Smith and Wesson Model 1891 thirty-eight calibre target pistol was in The Far Away Man's belt, under his coat.

He had seen him. He knew he was there.

In the park, The Far Away Man got up to go across the street.

There was no pain and all his muscles and joints were strong and supported him.

11.47 a.m.

The Far Away Man, unsweating, began walking without discomfort through the physical, diffusing curtain of heat.

4

On his way out through the Charge Room, Feiffer said, 'I'm going over to the Department of Health with the inoculation forms.' He had them safely in two labelled plastic evidence envelopes. O'Yee was gazing down at a police firearms manual. Feiffer said to no one in particular, 'I know what they're going to tell me but I have to ask anyway.' What they were going to tell him was that the pages could have come from booklets issued anywhere, at anytime, to anyone and there was nothing to be served in coming all the way over to ask about them. Feiffer, almost wanting to be stopped, said, 'I can't think of what else to do. At least it's something.'

It wasn't. It was nothing. He paused, waiting for O'Yee to offer him another suggestion.

There were no other suggestions.

O'Yee, nodding, wrote down the destination in the collator's book.

Feiffer lit a cigarette. The air was heavy and oppressive in the Charge Room.

In the heat, the cigarette burned his mouth and Feiffer stubbed it out in a crushed and distorted metal ashtray on the Charge Room desk and went outside into the street towards his car.

The last windjamming that had been done in the Victorian Windjammer Club had been in 1969 when it had been built and that was when the main doors to the Edwardian billiards room on the ground floor had been jammed by the wind.

Behind his mahogany-stained plywood desk, the Factotum of the club, a short balding man of, like the club itself, indeterminate European origins, raised his eyes to heaven and took a deep, cooling mouthful of smoke from a corn-cob pipe burning away in an ashtray out of sight under the counter. A club member was coming in through the main door: the Factotum got an ancient curved briar from the counter next to the corn-cob and stuck it in his mouth, let the smoke dribble out thoughtfully past the curved and silver mounted stem and, without actually saying a word, said, 'Good morning to you, sir.' He smiled deferentially.

The member, a tall, ramrod-straight man in his late seventies with a British-officer-in-India moustache, looked up at the clock behind the Factotum's desk.

The clock read exactly one minute to noon.

The member said, 'Hmm.'

The Factotum said – an octave lower – 'Hmm.'

The member said, 'Never wrong, are you, George?' He glanced at the pipe and the deferential, faint smile that secured it, 'Good old George.' The member said, 'Hmm,' and waited.

Just a touch more familiarity, just the faintest hint of knowing equality (after all, they were both about the same age so there was at least a common dislike of things that were not of the same age) . . . The Factotum said, 'Huh!'

The member said, 'Hah!' He glanced at the pipe, at the time, at the slight bow the Factotum made without seeming to move his body, and, satisfied, said, 'Ha! Good!' and went through the foyer towards the bar with a story to tell.

It was always the same story. The Factotum put down his empty briar and took a surreptitious puff on his corn-cob. Sent in from Kapp and Peterson's in Dublin and paid for by the Club Management, the briars cost over a hundred and fifty Hong Kong dollars each FOB. Bought locally at Wing's, the Tobacconist on Wyang Street, the corn-cobs cost eighty-five cents and, paid for by the Factotum himself, tasted wonderful.

Only another twelve months to retirement. The Factotum put down his corn-cob, brushed off his butler's waistcoat and pin-striped trousers, and took up his empty briar again.

He knew all the club members. They had a look about them. The Factotum, glancing at the door and seeing another member come in, put his briar quickly away and looked down at his hands. Except for a single adhesive plaster around the right index finger they were hospital clean.

The Factotum stripped the plaster off under the desk and, bowing a little from the waist, said quietly, 'Sir.' It was exactly noon.

'Still smoking that filthy pipe?' The second member was another tall, moustachioed ex-British-officer-in-India cut from exactly the same cloth as the first. This one had money. The Factotum waited and the man paused by his desk.

The Factotum said, 'No, sir. I took your advice and gave it up.'

'Hm.' The man, glancing around the foyer to see if anyone worth talking to was around, said, 'Filthy habit.' He tapped at his chest. In the overpowering heat he wore a midweight English tweed suit and carefully knotted regimental tie. The member said, 'Rolls-Royce quality. That's what the doctors say about my heart.' He leaned forward a little, 'Do you know how old I am this week, um –' he thought for the bloody man's name – 'Um, *George*?'

'No, sir.'

'Sixty-nine. Or if you want to do it the way the Red Indians used to, eight hundred and twenty-eight bloody Moons!' He pointed a bony finger, 'I only ever once tried tobacco and that was up with the Hill Tribes when we were being eaten by bloody mosquitos and, quite frankly, I came to the conclusion that I preferred the bloody mosquitos!' The member said, 'Don't doubt your word, George, but show me your bloody fingers.'

'Yes, sir.' The Factotum permitted himself a little smile. It had a touch of pride in it, but it was only the pride of achievement and that needing to be put somewhere between the two gauges of insolence and manly respect came firmly down on the credit side of the latter.

The member said, 'Stains your body, tobacco: inside and out.' He looked sly, 'Old Indian Army Intelligence trick: know what to look for.' He seemed happy, 'Pipe smoking leaves a stain on the index finger because of the way a fella holds the thing.' He looked carefully at the Factotum's plaster-white index finger, 'Now look at that for a bloody difference! Good man!' The member smiled, 'I've got nothing but respect for a man who knows when to take good advice.' He had money. 'You'll be all right at Christmas.'

'Thank you, sir.'

'Hmm.' For a moment, there was something in the member's face. He half smiled at it. It was his youth. The member, nodding, said for some reason he was unable to account for, 'Thanks very much.'

'Lieutenant-Colonel Rogers came in just a moment ago, sir. I think he's in the bar.'

'Good. Well done . . . um . . .'

The Factotum said, 'George, sir.'

'Well done, George.'

'Thank you, sir.' The Factotum needed a smoke. He waited until the man had gone into the bar still nodding to himself and reached under the counter for his corn-cob and got it burning again.

It was five minutes after twelve. He saw another member come in, walking slowly and carefully in through the open doors to escape the heat, and he put down the corn-cob for his briar and got himself ready for yet another brief, welcoming, predictable conversation.

On Beach Road, Feiffer sat in his car with the windows rolled down looking out at the moored junks and sampans flitting between them on the harbour. There was a slight swell to the water and he watched as the black hatted Tanka women made little white flurries with their stern-mounted oars and sent their sampans scudding through it.

All the sails on the junks were furled. In the heat they looked hard and dry and bone white.

U Ne (8.1.47). Koo Teh-cheung. (6.7.51).

The Department of Health would be able to tell him nothing.

12.06 p.m.

Stubbing out yet another too-hot cigarette in the dashboard ashtray, Feiffer sat in his car watching the boats.

In Kamikaze Mansions, The Human Poached Egg, still staggering a little from his recent cremation, said in a strange, sad voice, 'Bill, why are we doing this?'

Spencer said, 'It's a nuisance. People have been complaining.'

'Oh.' That seemed a good enough reason to die. Auden, still staggering, said, 'Oh. Good-oh. What do we do now?'

Spencer still had the calculator in his hand. He put it out of sight in his shirt pocket. Spencer said, 'Now we'll just have to try something else.' Nothing stopped him. He took the calculator out again and gave it a rub with his shirtsleeve. No genie appeared. Spencer said reassuringly, 'Don't worry, I've got lots of other ideas I haven't even tried yet.' He smiled encouragingly.

Auden said, 'Oh.' For a moment back there he had thought he had heard three thumps as three bodies had hit the ground. He had to be wrong. Ears were notoriously unreliable. They burned so easily. Auden said, 'I'm really sorry about the guns. I won't ever do it again.' He leaned forward for Spencer to pat him on the head.

Auden, reeling, not quite knowing what exactly he was predicating the sentence on, said with real regret, 'You know, it seemed like such a good idea at the time.'

He shook his head and, if there had been a single drop of moisture left anywhere in his desiccated, ruined body he thought he might have put his head on Spencer's shoulder and cried.

*　　*　　*

He knew all the club members. They had a look about them. Behind his mahogany stained plywood desk, the Factotum touched at his briar and then put it down again. There was the faintest wisp of smoke coming from the corn-cob and he put his thumb over it and smothered it. He glanced at the wall clock behind him. It was six and a half minutes after twelve. The Factotum, gazing at the member crossing the foyer towards him, looked down at his waistcoat and pinstriped trousers to see if there was a speck of something on them he should wipe off.

There wasn't. He knew all the club members. They had a look about them. It was something about the way they carried themselves: an air of authority, past or present: something about the way their eyes met yours without actually registering your presence until for some reason *you* had to provide, your presence was worth registering.

The Factotum, without seeming to move, made a little bow from the waist. He only had twelve months to retirement.

Something unnerved him and he stopped the bow and brought himself up a little straighter.

Some of the members had money.

The Factotum was staring at the member: there was something about him . . .

The Factotum said softly, 'Sir –' He produced the faintest of smiles: subservience mixed in with a little warmth. The member was in his mid-forties, too young for familiarity: the Factotum touched at his waistcoat with his thumbs and butler-like, clasped his hands together on his chest. There was a spot of something on the member's mouth. It could have been blood. The Factotum, leaning a little forward to show concern, said again, 'Sir –?'

The member was limping slightly: maybe a wound from one of the colonial wars of the mid-fifties or– The Factotum took his eyes away from the spot of blood so as not to embarrass and counted the seconds as the man came slowly towards him.

The test of an outsider was that he paused in the foyer and looked around and marvelled at the place.

44

The member came towards him with pale blue eyes seeing nothing.

He had not registered the Factotum's existence. The Factotum pursed his lips slightly and waited.

The amusing village idiot bit. The Factotum, glancing at the clock, said with a dull look on his face, 'Good morning.'

He got no reaction.

He was not a member. They all knew his little jokes. There wasn't one of them who didn't stop and share one of his little jokes or pass the time of day with him, or – The Factotum's hand moved on the desk to rest on that most potent of weapons: the membership book. The Factotum, standing straighter, said firmly, 'Now, look –'

'*George*.'

The Factotum said, 'Yes, sir!' The single word had that authority. It was familiar. It was a command. The Factotum said, 'Sir?' Whatever anyone ever said about the levelling of socialism, the ruling class *was* different. With the temperature outside in the high nineties there was not a single drop of sweat on the member's face. The spot on his mouth was probably just something from a good lunch. The Factotum said, 'At your service as always, sir.' He was a member: he simply couldn't place him.

'*Sharwood*.'

'Mr Sharwood is in the newspaper room.' He almost said, 'The Honourable.' Sharwood was the son of a peer, a baron, but that would have meant referring to him as 'Lieutenant Commander The Honourable Julian Sharwood', and that inference – that a mere Factotum would know an aristocrat's first name – with only twelve months to go before retirement would simply not do. The Factotum, knowing the member knew the way, trying to be helpful, indicated the corridor to the newspaper room. He took up his briar, 'Still smoking the old chimney, sir.' He smiled.

The Far Away Man's eyes were so pale as not to be there. On his face, in the torrid weather, there was not even a single drop of sweat. The Factotum said again, in case he had not been fully audible, 'Newspaper room, sir.'

He knew all the club members. They had a look about them. The membership book was on the desk in front of him.

As The Far Away Man turned to go towards the newspaper room, the Factotum laid his hand on it, but he thought the man might suddenly turn around and he took his hand away and looked down deferentially under his counter.

His corn-cob was there, extinct.

As he tried to get it alight for a quick, comforting smoke he could not understand why his hands were shaking and, suddenly he felt a little cold.

In the cellar, Lim said happily, 'I've done one, sir.' He held up what looked like a Broomhandled Mauser, 'I had a lot of trouble getting some of the internal bits together but I finally managed to get all thirteen screws into it and it seems to work just fine now.'

O'Yee, with a sad smile, said quietly, 'Oh. Well done.'

'Thanks.' Lim, flourishing the giant black gun said happily, 'You were right about man's viciousness and aggression, Christopher. Looking at this thing I can see it's an object of enormous power and danger to all around it.'

He couldn't bring himself to tell him. O'Yee, still smiling sadly, said, 'Did I say all that?' He thought of all the time he had spent with the firearms manual upstairs, and looked down at the hundreds of bits of guns still on the floor. All wasted. Lim said, 'Sir, how little man has learned.'

Too true. There were no screws in the internal workings of a Broomhandled Mauser. A masterpiece of late-nineteenth-century German engineering, the only screw in a Broomhandled Mauser was the one that secured the Mauser to the broomhandle: a tiny one-eighth-inch worm holding the wooden grips to the butt. As Lim drew back on the pistol's bolt and cocked it with a Snap! Man had not even learned to duck, and as O'Yee shouted in sudden terrified panic, 'Oh, *no*!', the pistol, flying to pieces with suddenly released Teutonic vigor, almost scythed them both down where they stood with each of its twenty nine badly assembled, screw-raped, mangled, lost forever in the junkyard bits.

Behind his desk, the Factotum waited with a vague sense of unease. He glanced towards the open door to the street, but there was no one else coming in to the club and, denied words, he was left alone with his thoughts.

It was twelve fifteen and a half.

The Factotum had an urge to stretch his legs. He glanced across the foyer to the doors and corridors leading to the members' rooms.

He knew all the members of The Windjammer Club. They had a look about them.

The Factotum, with only twelve months to go before retirement, was not a member of the club and, unless on business, all the rooms were denied to him.

He had never questioned his life before, but, alone in the foyer, behind his mahogany stained plywood desk, for some curious reason, for the first time, nigglingly, he began to wonder.

Sharwood, Julian John, (Lt-Cmdr. The Hon) b. Collon, Co. Louth (Ire) 19.7.38, f. Rt. Hon the Baron Chambreton (title created 1512) m. Barbara, the Lady Chambreton (nee Booth-royd, b. Berkshire, England); Eton 1944–50, Harrow 1951–58; Commissioned Royal Navy, 1960. Service Med 1961–3, Far East 1963–68, Administration and Stores, Far Eastern Station, Singapore, 1970–75, detached service Malaysia 1976 –80. Present posting, liaison Combined Stores, Hong Kong.

Single. Clubs White's and Windjammer, Hong Kong.

Decorations Good Conduct, Long Service, Malay Order of Merit For Valuable Service.

Recreations Sailing.

In the newspaper room, Sharwood, in lightweight civilian clothes, returned the *Straits Times* back to its place on the newspaper rack and ran his hand across his mouth. With the overhead fan going in the airy room he felt cool and at the same time a little tired around the shoulders from the change in temperature from the street.

He had a long, king-size menthol cigarette in his hand. He drew in on it and felt the smoke bite sharp and cold against the back of his throat. The cigarette made him cough. He looked down at it, considered asking one of the members in the other rooms for something stronger, thought of his health, and smiled to himself.

One thing the Royal Navy taught was self discipline. Sharwood, shaking his head, moved a copy of the *Times of India* and looked for another Malay or Singapore newspaper. The *Straits Times* he had been looking at was a day old: this morning's editions would not be in on the plane until after one. He turned away from the newspapers, looking down at his cigarette, and said with a slightly embarrassed smile to the man standing in the doorway watching him, 'You'd think the papers here had to come by bloody row-boat!' He crossed the room to a circle of cane chairs and glass topped coffee tables by the picture window that looked out onto the little park across the street, 'You'd think if they were going to tart up an old bloody brothel or whatever it was and turn it into a seafaring gents club they'd at least have had the decency to get it to look out onto the bloody sea.' The man at the doorway was making him nervous. He was talking more than naval discipline encouraged. Sharwood said, 'Sorry, did I have your paper or something?'

The man came a few steps into the room. Sharwood said curiously, 'Do I know you?'

The Far Away Man smiled.

Sharwood said, 'Yes, I know you. It's been a while, but we know each other, don't we?'

The smile went and The Far Away Man's face became still. There was no sweat on his face. The eyes were pale and far away.

Sharwood said, 'The other papers won't be in until one.' He nodded in the direction of the rack, 'All they've got is yesterday's *Straits Times*, but, um, nothing else –' He looked hard at The Far Away Man's face and tried to place him.

The Far Away Man went on looking at him.

Sharwood said, 'Um –' He watched as the man's hand went under his coat and touched at something on his belt. He saw a spot of something dark at the corner of the man's mouth. It looked like blood. Sharwood said, 'Are you all right? You look a bit ill.' The cigarette in his hand burned at his skin and he leant forward quickly and stubbed it out in an ashtray on one of the glass coffee tables. Sharwood said, 'Who the hell are you?' Sharwood said suddenly, 'Why the hell don't you say something?'

The Far Away Man's face was still. Below his eyes, as Sharwood stared, a shape rose, held in the shadow of two clenched fists. Sharwood saw it glint between the fingers.

Sharwood said, 'Oh, my *God*!'

The focus apex of the shadow in The Far Away Man's hands was the monstrous, staring, black muzzle of a pistol.

Sharwood said, with his hand still on the cigarette, crushing it out in the ashtray, 'No! *No!*' as The Far Away Man, unblinking and unsweating, shooting for a point midway between the second and third shirt button below his collar, pressed the trigger of the glittering gun and, instantly, blew him backwards over the table.

There was a sudden sound from behind him in the foyer as if someone had dropped a large book from a desk and then a flurry of voices, but The Far Away Man did not turn to see what it was.

Putting the gun back carefully in his belt and looking at Sharwood not at all, with easy familiarity he crossed the deserted newspaper room at the same, unhurried speed he had entered it and, turning into the corridor that joined it as an access went out through the back door of the building and into the street.

It was twelve twenty-one.

In Icehouse Street, as he walked, the heat affected him not at all.

5

Old Hundred Names was at it again. On the roof of the apartment block, Spencer, making the sort of clucking noise you made when you wanted a horse to giddyup, said in a lull in the racket, 'You have to admire them.' He made a clicking noise.

The Indefatigable Sleuth of Kamikaze Mansions was obviously taking time off to charge up the little grey cells. Auden said unenthusiastically, 'Yeah.' He actually heard what Spencer had said. He touched at his ear in surprise. Auden said, 'Who?'

'Them. Old Hundred Names.' Spencer nodded in the direction of the far corner of the flat roof, past the deserted netball court, to where the posse of Chinese vendors were replenishing their carts from boxes of sugar cane, cylinders of blancmange ingredients, vats of soy bean drink and boxes, crates, cylinders, vats and vessels of other, unidentifiable wares to cool and delight the residents of high rise buildings on hot days. Spencer said, 'Old Hundred Names: the Chinese labourer – the worker.' He clucked and clicked. He was not charging the grey cells, he was becoming positively ponderous. Spencer said, 'The people who built the canals and the Great Wall Of China, the strivers, the labourers in the vineyard.' (Auden said, 'They don't have vineyards in China.') 'The poor, unsung, unheralded working stiff who served the Empires, the Republic, and now –' Spencer was smiling at them benignly as they went about their unending task of keeping starvation and death at bay. Spencer nodded. It wasn't grey cell recharging time or ponderous time, it was Calvinist fix time. Spencer said, 'Don't they make you feel guilty at even the faintest *glimmering* of giving up?'

Auden said, 'No.'

Spencer, quoting something that sounded like a movie recommended by the Working Mothers Of America said with a catch in his voice, 'They Were Indomitable.'

They may have been. He wasn't. Auden, touching at his ear and feeling only embers, said, 'You really love this, don't you? You really think this is the ant's pants!' He looked at the Eternal Chinese at their work and failed to see what Spencer saw in them. Auden said, 'Look, be reasonable. We've done everything we can do! High-Dive Henry's already driven eight bloody Uniformed Men mad and we're next!' He looked to see if he had Spencer's attention. He hadn't. Auden said, 'And what have we achieved? What we've achieved is nothing!' He began counting on his fingers. The fingers were blackened. 'One, we've hung around on the ground there baking our asses off for bloody hours listening to that bloody maniac scream and jump and found nothing, right?'

Spencer was breathing shallowly. That was a bad sign. It meant he was still admiring.

'Right. And then, two, we hung around on the first few floors, looking about, and again, we found nothing. *Right?*'

Spencer, smiling gently, said, 'Right.'

He hated it when Spencer smiled gently. Auden said, 'And now, we've been up on this bloody roof frying our brains out and, again, we've found – what?' For an awful moment he thought Spencer was going to say 'Salvation'. Auden said, 'Nothing! Nil! Zero! Zilch! *Zip!*' It was absolutely no use trying to talk to Spencer when he was in one of his moods. Auden said, 'I don't know about you, but I think I've suffered enough to make even bloody O'Yee happy!' He took a step towards the stairs. His ears hurt. Auden said desperately,

'Look, all it is is a bloody nuisance. It's not as if he was a mass killer chucking people off balconies and bloody roofs in a cape and laughing like bloody Boris Karloff about it!' (He was almost going to say, 'If it was, I'd stay.') 'What he is is some stupid bugger – it's probably just some *kid* – who gets his kicks making shrieking noises and chucking things down to the ground –'

Spencer said, 'What things?'

'Invisible things!' Auden said, 'How do I know? And the reason it's a bloody nuisance is that every Chinese Hundred Names lunatic – you know, the bloody canal builders and the labourers in the vineyards of life – turns his fucking stereo up full blast as soon as he hears it to drown it out!' He had found the flaw in Spencer's philosophy: canal builders and vineyard labourers didn't have stereos. 'All it does is disturb their bloody enjoyment of their bloody videos and home movies, half of which are probably one hundred percent obscene and should get them fifty years in the bloody clink anyway! See? That's why they stay in their apartments when we're around: they're afraid we're going to bloody arrest them!' The heat was turning his brain to porridge. Auden said, 'I've suffered enough. I'm going back to the Station now and even if it takes me the rest of my life I'll put each and every one of those guns back together again!' Auden said the final argument, 'We're being turned into the Incredible Melting Men just so a few idiots can enjoy their home bloody video snuff and groin movies!'

Spencer said, 'Hmm.' He nodded.

Auden said, 'Did you nod?'

Spencer said, 'Hmm.'

Auden said, 'You'll never regret it, Bill.'

Spencer said, 'Hmm.' He nodded.

'Can we go now please, Bill?'

'Yes.' Spencer nodded again.

Auden said, 'Thank you.'

Spencer said, 'Hmm.' He was still nodding. The home videos, the stereos, The Home Jackhammer Course, part one . . . Spencer said, thoughtfully, 'You know, all High-Dive Henry is really doing is interfering with the noise level around here . . .'

Auden said, 'That's right!' He glanced quickly at Old Hundred Names on the far side of the roof. They were all right. He supposed if you got to know them, they were OK . . .

Spencer said, 'So that's what we'll do.' He stopped nodding.

Auden said joyously, 'Right!'

Spencer said, deciding, his little eyes all agleam with new determination, 'We'll go back downstairs to the concourse, to the switchboard, and then next time he jumps off the building to kill himself we'll turn off all the power to all the stereos and all the videos in all the apartments and hear exactly where he falls!' Spencer said, 'Phil, you're a genius!' He looked at the coolies. Spencer said happily, 'My God, Phil – what a marvellous challenge it all is!' For the first time, he looked at Auden.

Spencer, punching him lightly on the shoulder in pent-up anticipation, said, 'Aye? Don't you agree? By God, it's the only thing that makes life worth living, isn't it?'

He seemed very happy, at peace, consumed at once with the striving of The Common Man, infectious in his ethos of –

Auden, touching at his ear, said, 'Oh!'

Words failed him.

Auden said, 'Oh . . . *no!*'

In the newspaper room of The Windjammer Club, the Factotum, in tears, said for the third time, 'I tell you, I knew him!' He looked across to where Macarthur and the forensic team were working out of sight behind the overturned table where Sharwood had died, 'He came in here like a member and I *knew* him!'

'Then who was he?'

'I don't know who he was!' The overhead fan had been turned off in the room to keep down the dust and the Factotum brushed at his forehead with his hand. His hand came away wet. The Factotum shook his head as a flashbulb went off behind the overturned table and lit up the rivulet of blood that came out of Sharwood's body and flowed across the room to terminate near his feet. 'You have to understand: this is a club for gentlemen. You can't ask a man if he's a gentleman. You just know he's one because you – you –'

Feiffer said, 'What? Recognize his gentlemanly qualities?'

'Yes!' Twelve months. He had only had twelve months to go. The Factotum, swallowing hard, said again, 'Yes! That's exactly what you do!'

'How?'

The Factotum retreated into the safety of tradition. The Factotum, standing a little straighter, said evenly, 'If you have to ask no one can ever explain it to you.' It was the sort of thing, over the years, he had heard members say again and again. 'Can you understand that *at all*?'

The cane furniture was poor, cut-price work. Near Feiffer's hand there was a chair with a round headed nail sticking out of it. Under the nail, the cane was splitting. Feiffer pushed the nail back into the wood with his thumb. The cane had been stained to look old. The stain came off a little on his thumb.

The Factotum brushed at his waistcoat. He always brushed at the same spot and it shone. Like the chair, it was of poor quality. The Factotum said desperately, 'Apart from calling me by name, he only said one word to me! He said "Sharwood."'

'A question?'

'A statement.' The Factotum said, 'The way they talk.'

'And then what?'

'And then nothing!' The Factotum wanted to get away. The Factotum, running his tongue across his lips, said, 'The way they talk! *At* you! Not to you, *at* you!' A lifetime. The Factotum said, 'I'm talking about a lifetime – can you understand that? I'm talking about a routine, a habit, something recognizable!' He looked hard into Feiffer's face and tried to see understanding there, 'I'm talking about something understood.' The Factotum said, 'If he wasn't a member of this club, he was a member of one just like it!' He shook his head, 'No, it was this one –' It was impossible, he couldn't get it across. The Factotum said, 'I tell you, I *knew* him!'

'Then why didn't you question him?'

'Because he —' Behind the overturned table there was an awful noise that sounded like a chicken's chest being opened with a sudden wrench. The Factotum felt bile rise. The Factotum said, 'Because he —' The Factotum said to the unreacting man, 'God damn you, can't you understand what I'm saying?'

'Perhaps I'm not a gentleman.'

'I didn't mean that!' He saw the faintest of smiles at the corner of Feiffer's mouth and knew the man didn't give a damn about the label one way or the other. The Factotum said, 'I didn't question his right to be here because he obviously had a right to be here!'

'What right?'

'I don't know!' His job was gone for sure. The Factotum said, ' "Sharwood." Not "Mr Sharwood or "Commander Sharwood" or — he came in here and he simply said "Sharwood", and I told him Mr Sharwood —'

Feiffer said from his notes, 'He was a Lieutenant Commander in the Navy, wasn't he?'

'He was in mufti. In civilian clothes you always refer to a gentleman not by his rank but by —' He saw the faint smile again. The Factotum said, 'Mr Sharwood was an aristocrat. When someone asks for a titled person in the right tone of voice, you don't challenge him because you don't know who he could *be*!' The Factotum said quietly, 'All right, I was frightened to ask. All right?'

'All right.'

'It isn't all right!' The Factotum said, 'You don't have to grovel to people and I do! It's my life!' The Factotum said, 'And now it's over and what the hell am I going to do now?'

The fingerprint man was by the newspaper rack. The Factotum's eyes were still on the blood. Feiffer glanced at him and the man shook his head. 'Did he touch anything? Your desk or maybe —'

The Factotum shook his head.

'And in here?'

'Mr —' The Factotum changed his mind. The Factotum said,

'If I'd come in here Mr Sharwood would have thrown me out.'

'Why?'

'If you have to ask –'

Feiffer said, 'I am asking.'

The Factotum went cold. He shrugged. The Factotum said, 'Because of who I was.' There was a twist at the corner of his mouth. The Factotum said, 'Because I was – because I was a bloody servant! All right?' The rivulet of blood was flowing out from behind the table. If it was blue it didn't look it in the light of the police photographer's flashbulb and the white coat of the pathologist ripping its retaining flesh apart. The Factotum said, 'He would have chucked me out because the man who came in here was one of his own kind: a club member – and no, I don't know who it was and I've looked in all the bloody membership books and I still don't know who it was, and, no, I –' The Factotum said, 'He would have chucked me out because like all the dried-up, worn out, penniless bastards who come in here posing and pretending to be something in the twentieth century that died out in the nineteenth he needed to make himself someone by making someone else feel no one!' The Factotum said in the final anger of fifteen years of corn-cob and briar pipes and little jokes about the time, 'What sort of man is it who – of his own bloody choice – elects to be a fucking *servant*?' The Factotum said, 'Me! A bloody pathetic, second-rate bastard who hasn't got the courage of his convictions to be what he is but wants to be something that doesn't even really exist!' The Factotum said with a strange, satisfied look on his face, 'In England, now, all the aristocrats are turning their castles and their big houses into zoos and holiday camps. What do you think of that?'

His life was over. It had been a joke. Everything he had ever done or worked for– The Factotum, seeing the blood flowing across the floor, ordinary, dark, *dead* blood, said in a final little joke about the time to the gentlemen, 'Too bloody late for you, Mr Sharwood! Too bloody late for you!'

A flashbulb went off behind the overturned table and the Factotum, the tears flowing freely down his face and onto his shiny nineteenth-century-style cut-price waistcoat, said on his own account, the first true and real thing he had said within the precincts of the club in the last fifteen years, 'Fuck them! *I'm only sorry he didn't kill them all!*'

It was 1.30 exactly and, somewhere, in the city, The Far Away Man, still unidentified, still walking, still . . .

— Still had his gun.

'Arrgghhhh!'

On the ground floor near the corridor switchboard, Spencer, swishing down his hand like an artillery officer giving orders to instantly reduce Sebastopol, shouted, 'Now!'

Auden pulled the switch and every sound in all the fourteen storeys of Kamikaze Mansions died.

Auden said, 'Well?'

Nothing.

Spencer, listening, said, 'Wait a second . . .'

Auden said, '*Well?*'

Spencer said —

Auden said, '*WELL?*'

Spencer said — Spencer said, 'Well, whose idea was it anyway?

Auden said —

Nothing. Nothing heaped upon nothing.

Auden said —

Whatever he said was lost as in each of the four hundred and ninety apartments, on each of the fourteen floors, each of the — averaged out estimate — two thousand six hundred and ninety-five video watchers, cassette listeners, boat builders, radio freaks, washing-machine users, refrigerator door openers and, up until just a moment ago, air-conditioned tenants stuck their heads out of their doors and windows and began screaming.

Ears, knees, heart, mind. Auden, his humiliation complete, yelled back, 'SHUT UP!' but in the din, as High-Dive Henry threw himself to concourse thumping oblivion, this time not once but (count them above the racket) five times, no one heard a word and Auden, cursing and swearing to himself in silence, threw the switch in a shattering blue flash that almost electrocuted him and gave everyone back their own little share of goddamned, unearned, rotten, petty *power*.

The bit of gun that looked like a crankcase was no crankcase. It was a gun. In the basement, Doctor Death, getting into the swing of things, hefted the weapon and said with enthusiasm, 'Look at this, Christopher, I've looked it up and guess what it is?'

There were gun manuals and schematics everywhere. O'Yee said without any expectation of success, 'A pipe wrench?'

'It's a Webley Bulldog revolver chambered for the 0.577 cartridge!' It looked more like a cannon chambered for the nuclear apocalypse. Lim said, the neophyte conversion to the ranks of the gun nuts, 'Dirty Harry's forty-four magnum, nothing! This wasn't built to stop bank robbers! This was built in the last years of the nineteenth century to stop fanatical, juiced-up savages!' For one of the colonially oppressed he did the colonial oppressor bit as if born for the role. Maybe it came with learning English. He had a wad of telephone books set up against the wall of the room like target butts. He was gazing at them and making little whinnying sounds. 'I have to test it because I'm not sure I put the firing pin in the right way.' He turned the gun over quickly to disguise the fact that the firing pin was part of the hammer and there was no way to put it in the wrong way. 'There's a bag of rounds for it. No one will notice if I take just *one*.'

O'Yee paused. On the ground by Lim's feet was a little circular display of German Lugers. O'Yee had not realized they even had any Lugers. The Lugers looked like Lugers. O'Yee looked at the remaining mound of bits.

Lim said, 'I'm getting the hang of it, sir. I got the Lugers back snap, snap, snap – just like that.' He wanted a reward. Lim said, 'Sir, please, can't I test the dervish-stopper?' He was grovelling. 'I promise it won't be loud. I've got a few telephone books up to –'

What could you say? 'No'? Lim's eyes were gleaming.

O'Yee, regretting it the moment he said it, said, 'Yeah. All right. Just one. And just so long as it isn't too loud.' He glanced down at his watch to count the seconds off before launching. O'Yee said, 'OK then, when I count . . .'

The basement at Yellowthread Street Hong Bay became the attic of the Empire State. And then the Empire State caught fire and suffocated all ten million New Yorkers in the fumes. The room shook. The room lit up. The telephone books evaporated. The room filled with smoke. Part of the room caved in. No doubt, somewhere seismologists recorded a shock that they concluded in their notes had taken out four-fifths of South East Asia.

Lim, grinning maniacally, said, 'Wow!' He could understand why Auden had stripped the guns. He looked at O'Yee. Lim said in alarm at the sight, 'Too loud?' He looked at the smouldering wreck he had once been invited to call by its Christian name. Lim said in sudden, cringing contrition, 'Sorry, sir – too loud.'

O'Yee said, 'What?'

'Too loud!' The gun was still smoking in Lim's hand. He caressed it.

O'Yee said, 'Pardon?'

Lim said –

O'Yee, his eyes wide and desperate, bashing at his ears with his tiny fists, shouted, 'Aye? What? *Pardon?*'

Lim said, 'Too loud.' Well, live and learn.

He put the gun down gently on the ground and, spying something even bigger – it made Dirty Harry's magnum look like a *popgun* – Lim, with the mad gleam still in his eyes, went to get some more telephone books.

There had to be *something*.

There was nothing.

Behind the upturned glass, Macarthur had the contents of Sharwood's pockets laid out neatly to one side of the bloody chest. The shirt had been cut away and the wound swabbed clean for examination and the little circle of objects lay around the dark, gaping hole like souvenirs on some dead cannibal's bier. Macarthur said, 'That's it: one packet of menthol cigarettes, a box of matches, keys, a moneyclip containing . . . what?' He looked at his notes, 'Three hundred and fifty Hong Kong dollars and thirty Pounds Sterling, one military identification card, watch, signet ring, and second box of matches. That's it, no neck chains, coins, cufflinks, other jewellery or papers. The bullet went straight into the upper chest, into the heart and killed him stone dead where he stood.' He lit a cigarette, one of his poisonous French stinkbombs and blew smoke out. Macarthur said, 'I even checked his ears for ear-rings.'

Feiffer nodded. If there was anyone he could imagine who would have been less likely to affect an ear-ring even in these liberated times, it was someone like Sharwood. Macarthur said, 'The bullet's lodged somewhere behind the heart.' He touched at the wound with the index finger and the forefinger he used to hold the cigarette, 'I won't be able to get it out until I cut him up.' He looked down at Sharwood's shoes. They were suede, 'And if he had any dealings with a shoe shine man, it wasn't today.' He asked, 'Was it the same man?'

'According to the Factotum's description, yes.' Feiffer looked at the signet ring. It was a black onyx. He turned over the wrist watch: a stainless steel Rolex Oyster Perpetual and looked for an inscription. There was none. 'And according to the Factotum, he was a member here who the Factotum can't place and none of the membership books bothers to mention.' He looked down at Sharwood's face and was relieved to see the eyes were closed, 'I asked the Factotum if they ever had a shoe shine man in here and he said they hadn't.' There was no inquisitive look on Sharwood's face. The face was vacant – he had simply been wiped out in a single, dead centre shot. Feiffer said, 'Have you checked all his pockets?'

'What are you looking for?'

'What about his –'

'I've checked.' Macarthur said with slight irritation, 'I have done this before, you know. I'm sorry if it doesn't solve all your questions, but that's all there is.' He began to stand up. Macarthur said, 'It's hot. The sooner I get the body back to the Morgue the sooner I can –'

'Have you turned his pockets inside out or did you just –'

'I put my hands in and felt around.' Macarthur was becoming annoyed. He saw Feiffer reach down and roughly pull out one of the coat pockets. Macarthur said, 'I'll do it! It's my job and I'll –' It was the heat. Macarthur said, 'Listen –'

There was nothing. There had to be something.

Macarthur said, 'Listen, I know how you feel about this sort of thing, but –' He moved Feiffer's hand away and pulled out Sharwood's other coat pocket. It was also empty. 'Nothing.' Macarthur said, 'That's all there is.' He looked at Feiffer's face. Macarthur said, 'Look, I can't find you evidence that isn't there!'

'It can't be a psycho in this weather! In this weather –' In the room the heat was beating him down. Feiffer said, 'In this weather, nothing'll stop him and he'll just go on killing and killing!' There had to be something. There had to be something to do. Feiffer said, 'God Almighty, a shoe shine man and now this! He could kill *anyone*!' Feiffer said, 'I can't go on just going through the motions, there has to be something I can do!' He reached into Sharwood's trouser pockets and said in sudden hope, 'What the hell's this?'

Macarthur said, 'It's his handkerchief!' He wanted to get at the body before the heat did. Macarthur said, 'It's just a handkerchief that –' He saw Feiffer unwrap the bundle the handkerchief made and he saw something in the centre of it glisten in the light. Macarthur said, 'What is it?'

It was an ovoid box in the form of a spotted and striated cowrie shell, of some age, mounted with a silver lid engraved with a death's head and crossed bones and bordered by acanthus leaves. Feiffer said grasping at straws, 'It's a bloody snuff box!'

The death's head and crossed bones was the emblem of the 17th/21st Lancers, part of the Light Brigade who had charged at Balaclava. Feiffer, glancing down at the bloody shirt, said in final hope, 'He was a cigarette smoker. What the hell was he doing with a snuff box in his pocket?'

There had to be something. Opening the snuff box lid and taking out what, folded carefully three times, and pushed down hard, it contained, Feiffer said, 'Look!'

There had to be something.

There was.

It couldn't have been random.

It wasn't.

Unfolding the two sheets of yellow paper carefully secreted in the age-stained curve of the shell Feiffer said again in triumph, 'Look!'

   – OR REVACCINATION AGAINST CHOLERA –
   DE REVACCINATION CONTRE LE CHOLÉRA –
   Harada, Satoru (9.2.58).
   Yen Pei chi (11.4.62).

In the high, airless room, for a moment, it seemed the heat released its hold on him and, briefly, he was filled with hope.

Sharwood's eyes were closed and the face, blank in repose, unlike the shoe shine man's, seemed only as if it slept.

It was 1.37 p.m. and, entering the door of his fourth-floor apartment on Beach Road, The Far Away Man touched at his mouth with his handkerchief and brought away on it a single spot of blood.

Ah, the simple life.

Right about now, all the telephones in the Station were ringing red hot as (i) people complained about the noise, (ii) Special Branch complained about their guns, (iii) half a dozen building contractors complained about not being rung for the basement reconstruction job, and (iv) people rang to complain that all the Station phones were ringing red hot and they couldn't get through to complain.

Stone deaf from the gunshot, as, in the basement his able assistant Lim went about assembling and testing them on – probably, by now, live targets – O'Yee looked at his fingernails and took out his pocketknife to clean them.

He thought of his family living on his soon-to-be-granted total disability and invalid ex-cop one quarter pension and, sawing away at his nails in happy expectation of sooner or later reaching a vital artery, smiled at their happy faces in expectation.

He even thought of Auden, and, his mind completely gone, smiled at the thought of him too.

Ah, the simple life.

O'Yee, hiding his face in his hands, put his head on his desk and – simply – went into mourning.

THE FAR AWAY MAN

He hurt. In the main room of his fourth-floor apartment overlooking the harbour on Beach Road, The Far Away Man, on his knees in front of a glass topped coffee table, hurt.

CHARLEMONT, JEUNET ET NEVEU,
Rue de la Caserne, 16
BRUXELLES

The oak box holding the long-barrelled gun was open on the table. The Far Away Man put out his fingers to touch the label pasted inside the lid and his vision swam at the words and the etched border of strands of arms and scrolls that surrounded it. One corner of the interior of the 15″ by 8″ box was taken up by a triangular cartridge tray of twenty-five drilled holes: he touched at the tray with his fingers and felt the hard metal of the cartridges nestling there. They were in rows. He touched at one with his fingernail and it made a clicking noise as it contacted the one next to it. Twenty-three of the cartridges were still live. He touched at the two empty cases in their own separate corner of the tray and they made a different, empty, sound as they moved.

He hurt. On his knees, there was a dull aching pain in the small of his back and a sharp pulling on the walls of his stomach and he put his hands hard on the gun box and steadied himself until the pain went.

It stayed with him.

His chest cage constricted again. He put his hand to it softly and felt all the bones – they were frail, like the chest of a chicken. He took his hand away and touched at his mouth with his fist.

He felt blood. There was a long ebony cleaning rod set in with the other accessories in the gun box and he took it out carefully, concentrating on getting his fingers to work on it and screwed a little brass cleaning jag onto its end, inserted a patch, and, lifting up the gun to open its action, ran the jag once down the barrel to clean it.

He was out of breath. He caught a faint smell of residue from the barrel (the jag came out dark from the burnt black powder fouling in the barrel) and he sniffed hard to clear it from his head.

He was afraid to cough. Twisting his head, he put the rod back with the patch still in place.

He touched at the gun. There was a burning coming at the corners of his eyes and he thought he cried out with the pain, but no sound came. The interior of the box was lined in fraying blue baize. The Far Away Man touched at it with his fingers and felt its softness.

CHARLEMONT, JEUNET ET NEVEU,
Rue De La Caserne, 16
BRUXELLES

He touched at the label. It was a quality parchment, wonderfully engraved in old type, brown with age. A fragment came loose in his hand and he rolled it between his fingers and felt it turn back into fibre.

He thought he cried out with pain, but there was no sound.

Through the open picture window near the table he could see the sea. In the absence of wind, he could not smell its smells, but, far away, he heard the sound of a ship's engine on it, throbbing heavily. A gust of pain from his back twisted at him and brought his head down to the table and he thought he cried out, but, again, no sound came. He thought, for a moment, he heard the ship's engine stop.

There was no ship's engine. In the harbour all the ships were riding at anchorage and their sounds were all muffled by the heat. The Far Away Man, raising himself up with his hands, steadying himself on the gun box, swallowed and tried not to cough.

There was nothing else in the room but the gun box and the glass topped table. It was bare, like the sky through the open window, a single colour containing nothing. The Far Away Man put his hand on the fitted carpet near his knees and ran his palm back and forth across it until his fingers became hot with friction.

The Far Away Man said softly, 'What else can I do?'

No sound came. The room and the city and the harbour were silent.

The Far Away Man, hurting, closed his eyes and felt the pain coming. He touched at his eyes and they were dry. He thought, sometimes, he dreamed. He dreamed he loaded the gun. He dreamed he spoke. Sometimes, at night, he dreamed sometimes he was dreaming. He dreamed sometimes he woke from his dreaming and the dreaming was still there, and then . . . he dreamed again and woke.

All he had was the gun.

He thought he dreamed, but he put his hand back to the carpet and felt the heat on his fingertips.

He thought he cried out, but no sound came.

The Far Away Man, hurting, said, 'What else can I do?' In the empty room nothing was disturbed and he failed to know if he had said it at all.

The gun was lying to one side of the box, loaded. In his dream he had inserted the cartridge and set the weapon down by the box, ready. He heard, just for a moment, voices, and he turned his head.

There was nothing there.

He heard a single voice and he started and thought he woke

65

from his dream. He was awake or dreamed he awoke and there was no voice there.

The Far Away Man said with the burning feeling coming to his eyes, '*What else can I do?*'

He thought for a moment he put the barrel of the gun into his mouth and pulled the trigger.

The pain in his back and stomach twisted him down.

The Far Away Man said, with the feeling of tears in his eyes but no tears there, 'Tell me! What else can I do?'

There was no sound and no answer.

The silver gun was lying ready to one side of its 15″ by 8″ oak box on the glass-topped table.

The Far Away Man, rising from his knees with no expression on his face, took it firmly in his hand and took up a spare round from the box.

Once, everything had been different.

The Far Away Man, moving towards the door to the apartment and listening carefully for noises outside, put the cocked gun carefully into his waistband and felt not at all the pain in his back and around his eyes.

Once, everything had been different.

2.05 p.m.

With the big picture window in the room still open and running with condensation in the empty, unfurnished room, The Far Away Man, satisfied that there was no one outside, opened the door and went out quietly into the corridor and took the elevator down to the ground.

Once, like other men, he had even had a name.

No longer.

2.08 p.m.

The Far Away Man, in the street, touched at his gun.

6

In Kamikaze Mansions, High-Dive Henry was silent. In Kamikaze Mansions, Auden wasn't. In the centre of the concourse, looking up, glowering, his mortal frame a dripping mess, Auden said, 'Right. That's it. I've had it.' The racket from four hundred and ninety apartments going at full blast thundered down at him, 'I've been abused, humiliated, fried, shouted at, reasoned with, barbequed, and now near bloody electrocuted and I've had it!' Auden, brushing Spencer's restraining hand from his shoulder, shouted up at the apartments, 'The worm has turned!' It had not only turned it was about to do somersaults. Auden shrieked, 'You people just go on enjoying your degenerate bloody films and your lousy bloody music and don't you worry your pretty little heads over the fact that there's a fellow human being down here trying to help you who's getting the piss knocked out of him – *don't you worry at all!*'

No one was. Auden, hopping up and down and clasping his Python under his coat and then letting it go and then clasping it again, shouted, 'You go on digging your bloody canals and labouring in your bloody vineyards!' He saw one of the white-coated cart vendors on the first floor stop and look at him with a sugar cane drink in his hand. Auden shouted in Cantonese, 'And you, get on with your work!' Not only were the canal diggers and vineyard labourers having a real nice

67

time they were sipping sugar cane drinks and sucking at crushed ice bloody candies while they did it. Auden, still hopping, yelled, 'Go on, have a good time! Enjoy yourselves! That's all that's important in the world – be a success, and make a bloody fortune so you can lie around watching other people suffer!'

He saw Spencer start to take out his pocket calculator to correlate something else between High-Dive Henry and the cosmos and he tried to slap it down to destruction on the cement ground and missed. Auden said, 'No, this time we do it, not by bloody science and sociology, but by bloody policework!' He took his hand off his gun and looked around for something appropriate to policework, like a sledgehammer. Auden said, 'What we're going to do now is what we should have done in the first place – we're going to get rough!' He looked up to see the effect that one had on the sybarites. It had none. Auden, sweating and raving, said with a wild look in his eyes, 'We're going to huff and we're going to puff and we're going to blow your house down!' He looked around for some dynamite. There wasn't any. Auden, getting hold of Spencer's pocket calculator and shoving it back into his pocket, said dangerously, 'Right? *Right!*'

The calculator had gone into Spencer's pocket backwards. Spencer put his fingers in and turned the machine up the right way.

Auden gave him a look.

Spencer said, 'Right, right.'

'We've been reasonable, haven't we, Bill?'

The sugar cane drink vendor on the first floor looked hurt. Spencer, smiling at him to cheer him up, said, 'Well, I . . .'

'*Haven't we?*'

Spencer said, 'Yes! Yes! We've been reasonable.'

'We have.' Auden's eyes were going positively piggy. The positively piggy eyes were beginning to get a mad gleam in them. Auden, stepping forward as Spencer stepped back said, still touching at his gun, 'I appreciate what you've been trying to do for me, Bill. I understand that all this was just a way of making me get a grip on myself, well, now I have.' He put his hand on Spencer's shoulder and gave it a little squeeze.

Spencer, his face going white, said, 'Ahh!'

'Sorry.' Too hard. Auden, stepping back, said quietly, 'I understand what, in your subtle way, you've been trying to tell me. What you've been trying to tell me is that once a man like me lets a humiliation or a mistake get to him he's got nowhere else to go but straight down.' In that case, High-Dive Henry must have been the original Cantonese Joe Doakes. Auden said, 'But now I'm back in charge again and both you and the poor suffering citizenry I'm paid to protect can rest easy.' Auden said, 'Right?' His eyes didn't have a gleam to them, they were iridescent. Auden said, 'Right. Now let's go and get him.'

'How?'

Auden said, 'Right.' He looked up at the apartments with resolution. It wasn't his fault if he couldn't put the guns back together. It was just a question of time. With time, he could have reassembled every screw, each and every little spring and sear, every breechblock and barrel. With time he could have – Auden said, 'What do you mean, "How"?'

'*How?* How are we going to get him?' Spencer, reaching for his pocket calculator to count the ways, then, seeing Auden's face and thinking better of it, said reasonably, 'We've tried everything. We've tried listening and looking and –' Spencer said in a kindly tone, 'I'm glad you're feeling better, Phil, but to be honest –'

But to be honest? Auden said warningly, 'Yeah?'

'Well, I think we've tried just about everything.'

Hmphh. Auden said, '*Huh!*'

'Well, haven't we?'

'Huh-hmm.' Auden smiled. You could tell who you could rely on when the chips were down. In this world there were just some people who couldn't stand the strain. Auden said, 'Hmm, hmm, hmm.' He made a tutting sound. Auden, giving Spencer a little wink, said easily, 'No, of course we haven't. We've tried the ground and the roof and the sightlines and the soundlines and the corridors and the concourse but the one

69

thing he has to pass through: we haven't tried that at all!' He was looking positively maniacal. Maybe it was the heat. Auden said, '*Have we?*' He looked up at the apartments and then down to the ground and then up to the apartments again. He was saved. He was happy. He was himself again.

Auden said with a happy face and a gentle pat on Spencer's shoulder that almost calcified every bone in Spencer's body on the spot, 'Bill, think of this: think of thin air! Think of *a parachute*!'

It was the heat. The heat, at last, had cleared his brain. Auden, his face breaking into a wide, wild, mad grin, said with his arms out from his sides and flapping, '. . . Think of a giant *bird*!'

Shen. Sharwood.
  The Far Away Man paused in the street.
  U Ne. Koo Teh-cheung.
  Harada, Satoru.
  Yen Pei chi . . .
  Names.
  Shen. Sharwood. They were real.
  U Ne. Koo Teh-cheung.
  Harada, Satoru
  Yen Pei chi . . .
  They were nothing, just names.
  In the street The Far Away Man paused.
  The names on the Health Certificate pages he had once seen laid out on a table in front of him like playing cards were now no longer of any importance.
  Yellow. The pages had been yellow, all made out in the same hand. Once, there had been nothing more important.
  Shen, Sharwood: only they were important now.
  And Mao: grinning, gap-toothed Mao, born coincidentally with the same surname as the man who had once led six hundred million Chinese from feudalism to Communism, he was important.
  In the street, The Far Away Man paused.

He was a ghost, not real. The heat affected him not at all.

There was a single spot of blood at the corner of the mouth: he could feel its salt and warmth.

At 3 p.m., in Canton Street, The Far Away Man paused and wiped it away.

On the first floor of Kamikaze Mansions the sugar cane drink man was still standing against the railing of the veranda looking hurt. As a living symbol of all that Old Hundred Names had had to endure from one race of conquerors and barbarians after another, Spencer's heart went out to him. Maybe he could lip read. Spencer called out in Cantonese, 'No, it's all right, he didn't mean you should get on with your work, he meant –' He looked at Auden. Auden had meant him. Spencer said, 'He meant –'

Auden had stopped flapping. He was gloating. Auden, his agony all over, hunched his shoulders up to the back of his neck and, in ecstasy, said, 'Heh, heh, heh.' He had cracked it. It was all over. Good solid policework had struck again. Auden said, 'A parachutist or a giant bird!' He said, 'Heh, heh, heh!' He looked up at the sugar cane drink man.

The sugar cane drink man held up a drink. He wanted to make a sale. Spencer mouthed – Auden yelled, 'Fuck off!'

'One question!' Auden, still vibrating with joy and conquest raised a single stilling finger, 'A parachutist and a giant bird. Ask yourself, have you ever seen either of them land in the same spot *twice*? He asked, 'Aye?' Once you knew the method the solution was ridiculously simple. It didn't matter how many peasants you trounced on your way up to the castle, just so long as you fought your way through to the treasure room. Auden said, 'Aye? Well? Answer me!'

High-Dive Henry, your days were numbered.

Auden said, 'I worked it out, don't you see? He's jumping onto the same spot every time! That means he isn't jumping at all– That means he's already there!' Auden said, 'Don't you see? Don't you see? The giant parachuting bird makes it all

71

clear! He's not a man at all – he's a *gopher*!' He said in triumph, 'Yeah!'

Auden, glancing up and wondering why the sugar cane drink man wasn't applauding, got a comradely we-have-come-through hand onto Spencer's shoulder, and, turning Spencer's collarbone to dust with his grasp, said, happy, 'Well? Well? Well, *what do you think*?'

Auden, gleaming, said, '*Well?*'

'Lieutenant Commander Sharwood?' In the government-issue furniture filled office in the central nub of the Combined Stores complex off Aberdeen Road, Colonal Graham of the Austra-lian South-East Asia Stores Command said, 'Yes, I suppose you can say I knew him fairly well.' He was a large, tight looking man with a full head of copper-coloured red hair cropped short, 'I worked with him.' He was, like Sharwood, in civilian clothes: shirtsleeves and a tightly knotted regimental tie, 'And he was an unmitigated, first rate, solid gold – as our American allies would say – motherfucking son of a bitch.' He touched at his tie, 'OK?'

There was a little ebony stand at the side of Graham's desk holding what appeared to be three very ancient and corroded rounds of case shot. Below them, on the ebony, there was a written note: Case shot, Battle of Ironton, Missouri, US Civil War, obviously a gift from one of the American allies.

Feiffer said, 'OK.' Graham's hair, in the light from the picture window overlooking the warehouses and barracks buildings of the complex, went from copper to deep auburn and back to copper again. For some mad reason known only to Australians, red heads like him would always be known as 'Blue'. Feiffer said, 'And that's it?'

'And that's it.' The nice thing about being a soldier was that you weren't obliged to think well of people simply because they were dead. 'Lieutenant Commander Sharwood was a cocktail party sailor.' Graham, touching at the cannonballs and moving them slightly on their stand, said with no room for doubt, 'I'm Army. He was Navy and the closest he ever came to the sea was poncing around in that club of his and reading old yachting magazines that he got the bloody Mess to pay for.' He demanded, 'Clear?'

'And the two names on the Health Certificate pages don't mean anything to you? Harada and Yen?'

'No.' The pages, inside glassene envelopes, were in front of Feiffer on the desk with the snuff box.

'And the snuff box?'

Graham moved the cannonballs. 'Only that the crest looks like the 17th/21st Lancers.' He took one of the corroded rounds in his hand and, Queeg-like, squeezed at it. 'Either that or, more bloody appropriately to bloody Sharwood, the fucking SS.' Graham, growing visibly irritated with the conversation, said dismissively, 'I don't know. Quite frankly, I don't bloody care.'

'What did he do here? Sharwood.'

'Fuck all.'

'In theory?'

A second round joined the first in Graham's hand. Together, they made a grating sound. 'He did, in theory, electronics and weapons supply. He did the Royal Navy and I do stores and resupply for US Australian joint manoeuvres involving seaborne land forces.' For a moment, he seemed as if he was going to rise and terminate the questioning altogether, 'What he did, in fact, was oversee the non coms and the ratings to make sure they did everything!' Feiffer tried to guess his age. The face was lined, but from what he could see of the man's body behind his desk that was not. He could have been anything from thirty-five to near sixty. Graham said with the rounds still grating in his hand, 'OK?'

'I take it then that he never saw any active service?'

'Oh, shit!' For a moment Feiffer thought the man was going to laugh. 'Are we talking about the same man?' Leaning back in his chair, Graham made a clucking sound in his throat, 'Listen, the closest that bastard ever came to action was maybe one day when he tried to put on a pair of trousers that were too tight for him.' Graham said slowly and clearly as if he was talking to someone from another planet, 'Listen carefully, Mr Feiffer, I'll say it one more time so you can take it in: Sharwood was a shit. Have you got that? He was a grade A, fully paid-up, one hundred and ten percent *shit*!'

'He was some sort of aristocrat, wasn't he?'

Graham said, 'So was the fucking Duke of Wellington!' He leaned forward again and put the case shot back carefully onto their stand. He was getting patronizing. Graham said, 'Look, I know you hear all sorts of stories about Australians who hate bloody Poms, and even more stories about Australians who hate bloody aristocratic Poms, and even more about people who have been in combat who hate buggers who haven't, but that isn't even the faintest part of it.' He was not a man to explain. He twisted his face a little as if it was painful, 'But that wasn't the case at all. The reason I didn't like Sharwood was that he wasn't likeable.' He was still talking down, 'I've even got a Jewish acquaintance I don't like and, guess what, just like Sharwood, I don't like him for himself either.' Even with the overhead fan going it was hot in the office. Graham, touching at his forehead with his fingers, said at the end of his patience, 'I thought you came here for the truth. If you want a eulogy I suggest you try the Chaplain.'

'Look, I'm not trying to turn the man into a plaster saint –'

'Good!'

'– but what I am trying to do is find out who killed him!' It was hopeless, 'All I want to know from you is what sort of person he was –'

'He was a lazy, no-good bastard who got the bloody non coms to do his work for him, and then, if they screwed up, took their bloody names and put them on report and had them broken!' Graham said, 'Listen, I was in Viet Nam. I saw a lot of officers like him and I saw them get a lot of good men killed.' There was a scar just below the hairline at the neck that Feiffer had not noticed before. It showed white on the suntanned skin. Graham said, 'He wasn't in my bloody Army so I had to put up with him, but I put up with him as little as my duties made it humanly possible – all right? And now I'm not going to fall around in tears because someone's put a bloody bullet in him because if you want to know the plain unvarnished truth, if I'd had to take very much more of him I'd have probably put a bullet in him myself!' Graham said, 'No, no I wouldn't. What I'd have done is wait until he tried to blame yet another of his monumental fuck-ups on one of his bloody subordinates and I'd have taken him down a dark alley somewhere and cut his fucking head off with a rusty fucking knife!' Graham, going white with anger, said, 'There! Now you have it! *Anything else?*'

'Did he take snuff?'

'Did he – did he *what*? Probably!'

'But you've never seen the snuff box before?'

'No, I've never seen the snuff box before!'

'So, if as seems likely, he was carrying it around in his pocket –'

'Then he never took it out.' He glanced at the three rounds of case shot. 'And I don't have the faintest idea who the two names on the Health Certificates represent either! All I know is that –'

'What?' Feiffer said, 'What do you know?' Feiffer said with what appeared to be sudden anger, 'What the hell did he ever do to you?'

'I've told you what the hell he did to me! He made me fucking sick!'

'And?'

'And *what*?'

'And what *else*?' It was a risk, but he took it. Feiffer said fiercely, 'What else about him got up your nose? The fact that he was posted here out of the way because he buggered something up in England? To the bloody far ends of the Earth. Like you? The same way you were obviously chucked out of what? A combat regiment and pushed aside because you'd screwed something up?' Feiffer said, 'Where were you before this? Viet Nam? You're not the first Australian I've ever run across and I've seen this hard-nosed, aggressive bullshit act

75

before!' Feiffer said, 'Don't you come the officer-the-men-all-adore garbage with me, you just tell me –'

'I'm not coming anything with you!' For a moment Feiffer thought he saw Graham grin. Graham, no longer bored, said, 'What I'm coming with you, Charlie –'

Feiffer said, 'Harry. Feiffer. Mr Feiffer, or bloody Chief Inspector Feiffer, or if you're feeling really bloody well in your place, "Sir"!'

'Like hell!'

'And what do they call you back in the old cow paddock? Bloody "Blue"?'

'Not if they want to go on living!' Graham, the scar on his neck standing out lividly, said, rising, 'I've told you what I know! What the hell else do you want to hear?' He touched at one of the iron shot and twisted it against the tips of his fingers.

'What the hell else I want to hear is more than the fact that someone using the same gun, in the space of less than six hours, has shot and killed two people in the Colony who, so far as I can see, have got about as much relationship to each other as one of those little iron cannonballs and a fully armed B1 bomber!' He looked up at Graham and saw the man was shaking, 'I'm sorry you didn't like Sharwood, but as far as I'm concerned –' Feiffer, watching the man turn the iron shot over and over in his fingers, said quietly, 'Look, I'm sorry about the Viet Nam business –'

Graham said, 'Yeah.' He put the iron shot down and nodding, gazed out the window. The shot, on the ebony stand was wet with perspiration. Graham said, 'Talk to Warrant Officer Wong.' He nodded to the window in the direction of a group of sailors and Army men by a warehouse supervising the unloading of a truck, 'He was Sharwood's off-sider for a while between Navy Petty Officers. Ask WO Wong if you want to know any more about him.' He seemed on the edge of saying something. Graham, standing up, said quietly, 'Anything you want to know, you tell WO Wong I said it was all right.' There was something else. Whatever it was it was not going to come from him. Graham, wavering a little on his feet, said with a nod, 'Yes, you ask WO Wong and you tell him I said it was all right.'

The little iron ball was still on its plinth, silvered with moisture.

Outside, WO Wong had finished supervising the unloading of the truck and he was walking towards the office.

Colonel Graham of Combined Stores, Hong Kong, touching at the scar on his neck and gazing down at the glistening wet ancient round, said suddenly, 'All right? *All right?*'

Graham, shaking, said, 'Please! Please! If you want to know any more ask WO Wong!'

7

In Sharwood's bachelor quarters, Warrant Officer First Class Wong, drumming his fingers on the metal air conditioning unit by the window and gazing out across Combined Stores towards the warehouses and the administrative building said quietly in practised English, 'The late Mr Sharwood was a thief.' There was no room for discussion in his world. He touched at the crown insignia of his rank on his shoulder and turned to face Feiffer, 'Because of what he did both he and Colonel Graham have been under investigation by the Military Police for over seven months.' Sharwood's effects were still in the room: his pictures on the walls, collected objects, family photographs, and, just visible inside a partly open cupboard, his uniforms and civilian clothes. Wong glanced at them with distaste, 'Because of him, Mr Graham is still under suspicion.'

'I see.'

'Do you?' Wong said, 'Good.' He glanced at the partly open cupboard. 'Then you'll know that in a war, an officer like Sharwood would have been quietly shot in the back of the neck at the outset.' He faced Feiffer fully, a squat, enormously fit looking Southern Chinese in his mid-thirties, 'At the outset, in a war, the unit Warrant Officer or Regimental Sergeant Major would have seen to a man like Sharwood before the poison he carried around with him infected his whole unit.' On his chest, along with what looked like the ribbon of a Queen's Gallantry

Medal of the type awarded during the 1966 riots, Wong wore a Good Conduct decoration. Wong, earning it for the second time, said quietly, 'But there wasn't a war on and all that happened to Sharwood was that he was ordered to resign.' He shrugged. His manner was borrowed or copied directly from Graham's. 'He was due to go at the end of the month. That's all I know. The end. All right?' Even the accent had an Australian twang to it, 'If you want to know anything more about Mr Sharwood's effort at a military career I suggest you ask the MPs.'

'What did he steal?'

'He didn't steal anything.' Stealing denoted a certain physical effort. Wong said, 'He thieved.'

'What?'

'Parts. Bits and pieces of electronic equipment, money' – a twist came to Wong's mouth – 'some of it from the Non Commissioned Officers' Fund and some of it from – from anybody who didn't have his eyes on him twenty four hours a day. Personal objects, anything he could get his hands on.'

'Are you saying he was a –'

'I'm saying he was a thief!' Wong was breathing hard. His fingers drummed on the air conditioning unit obsessionally, 'I'm saying he covered his thieving by making it look as if it came from the top and I'm saying that when he knew the red caps were after him he planted some of the things he took in Colonel Graham's office and almost sent him down as well!' Wong said, 'What I'm saying is that Sharwood –' He stopped drumming. Wong said, 'You won't get any tears from me that someone blew his brains out, none at all.'

'What exactly did he take?'

'I've told you.' It was over, finished. Opinions were fixed and there was an end to it. 'Bits and pieces of electronic equipment, money and small objects of value.'

Feiffer said, 'Like a silver snuff box?' He had the cowrie shell box in his coat pocket. He took it out in its plastic envelope and held it out.

'No, that was his.'

'You've seen it before?'

'Yes.' Wong, ever the Warrant Officer, said warningly, 'Don't run away with the idea he was Fu Manchu the master criminal. What he took probably only amounted to what any decent hard-working man could make in a month on a building site. It wasn't the value that counted, it was the idea behind it.' He drew a breath. 'He wasn't like Mr Graham. He was cheap and petty and devious. He wasn't any sort of man at all.'

'And what about his petty and devious friends?' Feiffer said. 'At the club where he was killed he had a yachting magazine. Did he ever go –'

Wong said, 'What? Yachting? Who with? With the local Chinese millionaires and magnates?' He paused with a thin smile on his face, 'No. Mr Sharwood, he didn't like the Chinese and the Chinese didn't like him. As for the Europeans, for the Services, this is a small Colony and word gets around. It got around with him, and, unfortunately, because of him, it got around about Mr Graham.' He paused, gazing at the partly open cupboard, 'But we're going to fix that. Now that Sharwood's dead we're going to make very sure that everyone knows exactly what he was.' He looked back at Feiffer, 'I didn't kill him and neither did anyone I know, but if I was going to get someone to put a bullet in somebody's head Lieutenant Commander Sharwood would have been the one.'

'He was shot in the chest.' And if he had killed Sharwood or put anyone else up to it, he wouldn't be talking about it now. He was getting nowhere. There was nothing. Feiffer said in desperation, 'Do the names Satoru Harada and Yen Pei chi mean anything to you?'

'No. Who are they?'

'Or U Ne, or Koo Teh-cheung?'

Wong shook his head.

It was hopeless. It was all he had. Feiffer said, 'What about a shoe shine man named Shen?'

'Is that the one who used to come here to do Sharwood's shoes?'

'I don't know. Is it?'

'Yes.' Wong, thinking, said, 'Yes, that was his name. A wizened sort of man wearing sandals. He came here a few times. We took his name at the gate.'

'What about a tall man, a European, fair haired, with very pale blue eyes?'

'No.' He didn't have to think about that one. He would have remembered. Wong, shaking his head, said, 'No.' Something niggled at the back of his mind. Wong said, 'About those names – is one of them Japanese?'

'Harada, yes.'

'Because I've seen it somewhere, or I've –' Wong said, 'It was in his snuff box.'

'What was?'

'A –' He hadn't taken much notice at the time. Wong said, 'A – a –' He put his fingertips to his forehead to remember. 'A – a sheet of yellow paper, two sheets. One of them – I noticed – had a Japanese name on it: Harada. I noticed because –'

'*Health Certificate pages?*'

'Yes.' Wong thought back, 'It was a while ago, when I still thought Sharwood was innocent, before we found out – when I still had my good opinion of him as an officer.' He shook his head, 'I associate the name with the shoe shine man.' He turned and drummed on the air conditioner, 'And, ah –' Wong said suddenly, 'I came in here one morning to tell Mr Sharwood he was late for a meeting with the Colonel and he was in here showing the shoe shine man a sheet of yellow paper he was taking from his snuff box! I remember: they were laughing about something. I remember because Sharwood didn't speak Cantonese and yet he and the shoe shine man were laughing about something and he held up the sheet with the Jap's name on it and said to me in English, "You know what this is? This is freedom!" and then he asked me to translate what he'd just said and say it to the shoe shine man in Chinese.'

'And did you?'

'Yes.' Wong said, 'It was weird. The shoe shine man used to bring Sharwood copies of the *Straits Times* when he came to clean his shoes and when I translated what Sharwood said he reached over and touched that day's copy on the floor and just said –'

'What?'

Wong said, ' "Knifeteeth." He said it as just one word: "Knifeteeth." ' He looked hard at Feiffer's face. Wong said curiously, 'Why? What does it mean?'

It was the heat. Poor sod, he had gone mad. On the concourse, Auden, lugging a sledgehammer over from the car, gazed heavenwards and said, 'Hah!'

No, he hadn't gone mad, he had gone totally raving. Auden, swinging the ten-pound lump over his shoulder like a base-baller, said, 'Hah, hah, hah!' Auden, staring heavenwards, said, '*Gophers!*'

Completely and utterly bananas. It was sad. Spencer, look-ing away in embarrassment, said softly –

Auden said, 'Parachutists! Giant birds! Gophers!' The ear that he had burned off on the hot ground was throbbing a bright red. Auden said, '*Revenge!*'

O'Yee had a lot to answer for. Spencer, going forward with his hands outstretched to draw poor, over-punished Auden into the calming bosom of an understanding friend, said soothingly, 'Phil . . .'

The ten-pound hammer came down like Babe Ruth trounc-ing an umpire and tore up three square feet of the concourse concrete in a single blow. Auden shouted, 'Noise!' All around him the two thousand six hundred and ninety-five stereo players, video watchers and chainsawing boat builders were going mad. Auden, swinging the hammer again and almost taking Spencer's feet off at the ankles, yelled, '*More* noise! A chunk of cement went up in the air as if it had been hit by a grenade and, crashing down fifteen feet away, brought up another piece that looked as if it had been hit by a mortar bomb. That too, went sailing up. Auden yelled, 'The case of the dog that didn't bark in the night!' He swung the hammer, '*Bedlam!*'

'*Aaarrggghhhh!*'

It was High-Dive Henry. The scream sounded desperate.
Auden yelled, '*Silence!*'
He stopped pounding.
Auden yelled –
Silence. No thumps, no bangs, no falling bodies, in fact –
Auden yelled in triumph, 'Silence!' He went on pounding.
This was real police work.
Auden, happy hitting something, yelled, '*Victory!*'

'Knifeteeth.' It meant nothing at all.
In Sharwood's bachelor quarters, Feiffer, opening the last
drawer in the place and finding nothing, shook his head.
Presumably, in advance of its owner's departure, everything of
any significance in the room had been packed up and sent off,
and what was left, apart from a few family photographs and
decorative wall pictures of no value, were only the clothes
Sharwood would have needed to see his time out in the
Colony.
That and a snuff box with two yellow sheets of paper in it, a
carton of cigarettes, matches and –
– and a bullet in the heart.
In the room, Feiffer said quietly, 'There's nothing in here.'
He looked at Wong watching him.
Everything, including Sharwood and the shoe shine man,
was gone.
"Knifeteeth."
He had absolutely no idea what it could possibly mean.

In the Yellowthread Street Station basement, O'Yee, patting
Lim on the shoulder, said with a smile, 'I'm feeling better now.
My hearing has come back.' He was tottering. His balance
canals were still shot. 'I'm very grateful for all the work you're
doing down here and I can understand you wanting to aug-
ment your historical knowledge by shooting some of the guns,
but I think you should stop now.' The entire collection of
Station telephone books, going back to the time of the Opium
Wars, was confetti on the floor. O'Yee said, smiling, 'OK?'

OK. Lim, putting down some sort of lethal weapon that looked like a cross between a bazooka and an even bigger bazooka, said understandingly, 'Sure.' On the floor by the bazooka there was something else that looked like a rocket for the bazooka. Lim gave it a kick and it went over towards the centre of the confetti, made what for an awful moment O'Yee thought was a fizzing noise, and then rolled over onto its side and sulked. Lim said, 'I'm sorry about your ears.'

He was doing a good job. If you could manage to drag your eyes away from the bazooka rocket just lying there you could see he was doing a good job. Assembled guns were actually appearing on the floor through the forest of parts for guns. O'Yee said, still staring at the rocket, 'Oh, it's nothing. It goes with the responsibility of command.' The gun books and schematics were laid out all over the floor, covered in grease and thumbprints. O'Yee, trying to be encouraging, said with a smile, 'Um, found anything else as interesting as the dervish-killer?' He winced as Lim, in a single sweeping movement that would have left Billy the Kid dead on the bar room floor, produced a squat black gun from behind his back. O'Yee, trying not to cower, said, 'Gee, what's that?' His ears contracted in self defence against his head. O'Yee swallowing hard, said, 'Gosh, gee, that's a nice – um – that's a nice thing, isn't it?'

Baron von Krupp sparkled. Lim said, 'Yeah! It's a Japanese Nambu eight-millimetre type 94.' Before or after the Bomb had fallen? Lim said, 'It was made in the Japanese Nambu factory in about 1934 and intended for commercial export, but instead, adopted into the Japanese Army at the outbreak of World War Two for –'

O'Yee said, 'Don't touch the trigger!' His ears retreated for safety into a small, previously unknown cavity found at the back of his head. They peeked out from under his hair and folded themselves into little balls. O'Yee said –

'It was adopted in the year 2594 of the Japanese calendar which is why it's called the Type 94.' You could learn a lot with guns. Lim, swinging the horrible thing with his finger through the trigger-guard, said informatively, 'In the Japanese calendar, The Son Of Heaven would be –'

O'Yee said, 'Don't touch the trigger!'

'– would be –'

'*Don't touch the trigger!*'

'I'm not going to touch the trigger!' He was attempting to impart historical information. Lim said, 'Would be –'

'Don't touch the –' He was going to touch the trigger. O'Yee, wrenching it from him and pointing it safely at the ground, said with all his intentions gone for nothing, 'You stupid idiot, you were going to touch the *trigger*!' He put his hand firmly on the sear bar on the side of the gun and nothing was going to make him give it back.

'You don't have to touch the trigger!' Lim, sweeping his – thank God – unarmed hand in the direction of the gun books said in annoyance –

'You're damned right you don't have to touch the trigger!' Lim was advancing. O'Yee pulled the gun back protectively and held it up above his eye level. He held the gun in a grip of iron. He squeezed at the sear bar.

'You don't have to touch the trigger because it's a Japanese suicide pistol and all you have to do is squeeze the sear bar!'

O'Yee said, 'Oh.'

Oh Magoo, you've done it again.

Strangely enough, as the gun went off in a single blinding flash of light an inch from his face, the noise wasn't too bad.

In fact, with the front of his brain concentrating fairly fully on the suddenly transmitted information that both the retinas of his eyes seemed to have turned instantaneously to jelly, the noise came as only the most minor of petty annoyances, and the back of his brain where his ears were, bouncing off the inside of his skull two or three times in rapid succession, took almost no notice of it at all.

In the basement below the station, O'Yee, fumbling in his pocket for his glasses, or, better still, if there happened to be one anywhere around, a seeing-eye dog, said –

There was something to say.

O'Yee said it.
O'Yee said –
O'Yee shrieked, '. . . *AUDEN!!*'

Mao.

In Cuttlefish Lane, The Far Away Man traced the Chinese characters on the nameplate with his fingernail. There was nothing more on the wooden hand-painted sign: just the name.

The Far Away Man touched at the flaking paint with his fingernail. It was vermilion, the colour of dark, arterial blood. The Far Away Man brought a little speck of it off and looked at it on the end of his finger.

The sign was screwed onto the side doorway of an old two-storey office building. There were other signs above and below Mao's, also hand painted, also screwed into the wall, but giving more information about their owner's businesses and preoccupations.

The Far Away Man looked at the other signs not at all.

Stepping back in the street, he looked up at Mao's window.

Mao. It was also written on an opaque, frosted window upstairs. He saw the snout of a cheap air-conditioning unit mounted in a cut away square of the glass and, here and there in the grille, little bits of paper and rag and effluvia caught by the machine's intake as it worked. He was there. The Far Away Man stepped forward again and touched at the sign.

Shen.

Sharwood.

Mao.

3.39 p.m. In mid-summer, in Hong Kong, a little under three and a half hours until dark.

Time enough.

The Far Away Man moved off the street into the darkness of the doorway and waited patiently until his eyes adjusted to the focus.

Shen.

Sharwood.

Mao.

The Far Away Man weighed almost nothing at all and as he mounted the steps one by one, there was no sound and, on the upper floor where Mao's unadvertised single roomed office was, no one heard him coming.

On the phone, Spencer said urgently, 'He's gone mad, Christopher! I don't mean he's gone a little funny in the heat, I mean he's gone stark, staring, raving mad! He's out in the middle of the concourse with a sledgehammer drooling about catching giant birds in parachutes and feeding them to the gophers!' Spencer said, 'Can't you hear it?'

Yeah, he could hear it. He could also hear the sound from the basement as Lim, in an orgy of cordite, fought out World Wars Three and Four with handguns. That was all right too. O'Yee was a married man. He was used to people ganging up on him. It was a pity about his eyes, but there was always room at home in San Francisco for yet another blind, ethnic beggar. O'Yee said in a neutral voice, 'Gee whiz, is he suffering very much?'

Spencer said, 'Yes!'

O'Yee said, 'Hmm.' Blind, ethnic beggars would always have this to remember. O'Yee said, 'Well, I hope he's successful in all his endeavours.' The floor beneath his desk jumped a foot as, in the Third and Fourth World War, the warring parties decided to go nuclear.

O'Yee said, 'Well, thanks for ringing me, Bill, but I'm afraid my life has taken rather a turn for the worse recently and as much as I'd like to go on chatting to you like this for, oh, just ages –'

Spencer said, 'Hullo! Are you there?' For a moment he thought he had got a crossed line. He made a wincing sound as, in the Greenland dig, a piece of sod careered past his head and detonated against the wall of the side of Kamikaze Mansions like a cluster bomb. Spencer said, 'Christopher, are you there?'

The floor had settled beneath his feet. At his desk, O'Yee glanced at the condensation on the wall. Was it condensation?

No, it wasn't. The wall was melting. O'Yee, whistling a little tune as, using one of the assorted automatic weapons, Lim went on an orgy of foundation weakening, said, 'Yes, I'm still here. What exactly would you like me to do for you?' He was happy. His fate was settled. He was finished. O'Yee said hopefully, 'Anything I can do to help you along life's difficult path.' He smiled.

Spencer said firmly, 'Christopher, I want you to forgive him about the guns so I can take him home out of the heat!' He waited.

Home. Ah, home ... Sweet magnolia blossoms and the slaves humming in the fields, the ripe bursting tang of cotton in the air, the sound – ah, a long way across the next green hillock – of the square dance and the fife band. Ah, autumnal scenes of rural tranquillity and the feudal system – the peasants, the lords, the villeins, the lieges, and the village executioner. Oh joy it was then to be alive. O'Yee said, 'Sure. Why not?' Such a little thing. 'Anything you like.' He sighed. He smiled. His brain was still quivering, but there was no more pain. Ah, happy absence of pain. O'Yee said, 'I forgive them all.' He asked, 'Who are we talking about?'

Spencer said, 'Phil!'

Oh, *Phil*! That noble yeoman. O'Yee said joyously, 'All of them. Tell them I forgive each and every one.' He smiled knowingly. The South would rise again. O'Yee said, 'I am not one to hold grudges.' He asked, 'Phil who?'

Below him, the mantel of the world was being shot to pieces. The walls were melting. His desk kept jumping up and down. Funny about his eyes: the telephone seemed to be working OK but he just couldn't get a picture of it.

Spencer said, 'Phil! You know – Phil! Detective Inspector –! You know, the man who stripped all the guns in the basement: Detective Inspector Phil *Auden*!' Spencer said, concerned, 'Hullo? Hullo?'

Spencer said desperately as yet another piece of the concourse took flight from the sledgehammer and nearly took him off at the waist, 'Christopher?' Spencer, trying to be everyone's friend and making a hash of it, said, a little hurt, 'Christopher, why are you laughing like that?'

Knifeteeth. In the open doorway of the first floor, the Far Away Man saw Mao. He saw Mao look up from his table and gaze at him for a moment. The Far Away Man watched the man's face to see what he could read in it.

There was nothing but mild annoyance. The Far Away Man had changed utterly and Mao, thinking only that a European tourist had come accidentally into the wrong room, rose to re-direct him and recognized him not at all.

3.43 p.m.

Knifeteeth.

The Far Away Man had at least three hours in hand before dark.

8

Everywhere you looked it was a dead end.

On the phone in the Detectives' Room, Feiffer said with rising irritation, 'Yes, Neal, I have been on to the Military Police – I talked to someone in the Prosecutor's Department – and what they told me only confirmed what WO Wong told me, namely, that if Sharwood got himself killed over what he pilfered from Combined Stores then whoever did it had a bad case of the cheaps. What Sharwood took over the eight-month period, altogether, amounted to about the wage of your average coolie in a bad three-month season.' The Commander was trying to help, running it through bit by bit. Feiffer said, 'All the MPs could suggest was that if anybody killed him because of what he pinched it was probably the poor dumb bloody Colonel he tried to frame, but since the whole investigation and hearing seems to have turned him into a bloody near nervous wreck they doubt he could even have worked out how to do it, let alone actually have done it.' He thought for a moment of Wong, 'And the only other direct link to Sharwood wouldn't have got someone to stroll into a European gentlemen's club and shoot him with a nineteenth-century single-shot pistol; he'd have caught up with Sharwood and cut his head off with a piece of piano wire. And then smiled about it.' Feiffer said, 'No, whatever got Sharwood killed, it didn't have anything to do with what he stole.'

'You're sure?'

'No, I'm not sure!' There was nothing to be sure of. 'It's a professional opinion, a guess!' The desk and the walls in the Detectives' Room were running with moisture. 'There isn't anything else to go on but guesses.'

'And the Health Certificate pages?'

'I don't know. They're all written in the same hand, but since there's just a single torn-out page – torn out with loving care so as to avoid anything that might show where they were issued – they could have come from anywhere from here to Helsinki and at any time over the last God knows how many years. And since they've all been treated as if they were pages from the Gutenberg Bible and kept carefully folded in pockets or tucked up in little silver snuff boxes –'

'What about this snuff box?'

'It's a silver-mounted cowrie shell from about the early nineteenth century with the badge of the 17th/21st Lancers on it. It just doesn't make sense that Sharwood and the shoe shine man could have been the bosom buddies WO Wong claims they were, but there it is. And then there's "knifeteeth" – whatever that means.'

'In English, it doesn't mean anything. What does it mean in Cantonese?'

'It means "knifeteeth".' Feiffer had spent all his life in the Colony. If it existed as a word he would have heard of it. Feiffer said, 'It means "knifeteeth".'

'You're sure it wasn't a mistake, that WO Wong –'

'WO Wong doesn't make mistakes.'

'Then we're down to circumstances?'

'Then we're down to circumstances.'

'Which are?' The Commander, listing them, said, 'Fingerprints?'

'There was a single print on the doorhandle of Mui's shop, but according to Fingerprints it was too smudged in the heat to be read.' Feiffer rubbed at his face. Across the room O'Yee was putting eye drops into his eyes and blinking hard at the irritation. Feiffer said, 'And witnesses: we've got a grand total of two. One who says that the only thing he could remember about a man who stood in his shop for over half an hour pointing a gun at him is that the gunpointer wasn't real, and two, a Factotum at a gentlemen's club who says that he recognized The Far Away Man as a club member, but can't remember what his name is –'

'You've had him go through the membership lists?'

'I've had him go through the membership lists and the group photographs and the portraits on the wall and the bloody mess bills and the –' Feiffer said angrily, 'And every other god-damned thing I can think of in that bloody place short of his handwritten memoirs of a life in service!' It was not the Commander's fault. He was trying to help. 'Neal, all I've got is four pages from four Health Certificate books written in the same hand with four names on them who could be – who could be fucking *anybody*!' Feiffer said, 'Circumstances? I haven't got any circumstances! All I've got is a collection of bits and bloody pieces which, when you add them all up, amount to exactly nothing!' The phone in his hand was wet with perspiration. Feiffer said with an effort at evenness, 'The fact of the matter is that in just under six hours on a hot bloody summer's day two people have been shot dead by the same man for no apparent reason and then that man seems to have disappeared into thin air, and, for all I know, he could go on killing and disappearing the same way until the bloody cows come home!' It was useless. He was simply trailing The Far Away Man around picking up his droppings. Feiffer said, 'I can only assume from what Wong says that Sharwood and the shoe shine man were involved in some sort of arrangement together, but as to what the arrangement was I haven't got the faintest idea!' He was gasping in the heat. Overhead, the fan on the ceiling seemed to be doing no good at all. Feiffer said, 'I'm sorry, but there it is. *Nothing*.'

'What about this bleeding from the mouth business?'

'Macarthur at the Morgue says it could just be a cut lip.'

'Or what else?'

'I don't know.'

'Description?'

It was written down in Feiffer's open notebook. It was also written on the day sheets of all the squad cars. For all the good it was going to do it could have just as well been written on the water. Feiffer said, 'Blond, pale blue eyes, about six feet, thin build, forty to forty-five, lightweight grey suit –'

'That sounds like a hell of a lot of people.'

'That sounds like half the passenger list of every plane-load of northern European tourists who land in the Colony eighteen times a day, every day!' Feiffer said, 'Distinguishing marks –'

'None.' The Commander said –

'Wrong. Distinguishing marks a distinct lack of reality.' Feiffer, getting bitter, said in the heat, 'Go to it, lads, every tall European who doesn't look real, pick him up and get at him with the rubber hoses!' Feiffer said, 'Tall, fair-haired and blue eyes, thin build – Jesus Christ, it sounds like me!'

'What about what he said to –'

'He said – to Mui in answer to a question – "no." He said, at the Windjammer Club, "Sharwood."' Feiffer said, 'Circumstances: he isn't mute. Evidence: he speaks English. Inference: he's a man of few words. Evidence: He doesn't talk to bloody people, he shoots them!' He was losing control. Feiffer said, 'Look, Neal, if you want the bottom line, the bottom line is that he's a nice, neutral, perfectly camouflaged murderous little sod who isn't real who, for one reason or another, is going around shooting people.' At base, that was all there was. Feiffer said, 'He killed a man at half-past eight this morning and then another at a little after one this afternoon. It's now almost four and, for all I know, he could well be in the process of killing another one now!'

'With another two Health Certificate pages.'

'Yes, with another two Health Certificate pages! And for all I know, the next two Health Certificate pages could be made out to – I don't know – a bloody Nigerian and a Brazilian! Why not? So far we've got a Burmese, two Chinese and, for good measure, a bloody Japanese! Or, I don't know, he could be branching out and this time he could go for the owner of the pages made out for a bloody Afghan and a Russian – you know, keeping the connection all up to date for us.' Feiffer, at the end of his patience, said firmly, 'I know you're trying to help, but I've been through this all myself twenty times and it still comes out zero! I'm only sorry the late Dame Agatha Christie isn't with us anymore or she could have set it all in a house on the bloody windswept moors and, like *The Mousetrap*, it could have run on stage for thirty bloody years!'

'Do you want more help, Harry?'

'*To do what?*'

'To do –' There was a pause. The Commander said hopelessly, 'To do –' The Commander said, 'You're waiting, aren't you? That's what you're doing, isn't it?'

'Yes.'

There was nothing else to do. Feiffer glanced at the clock on the wall. Behind the blur of condensation on the face, the hands read 3.49 p.m. Feiffer said, 'Thanks anyway.'

The hands moved a single click.

3.50 p.m.

In the Detectives' Room, he was doing all he could.

He was waiting for The Far Away Man to kill again.

3.50 p.m.

It seemed the face of the clock, behind the glass, inexorably, was drowning in its own moisture.

In his little room on the first floor, the European had sat down. Mao, twisting his face slightly, said slowly and clearly, 'Um . . . nei gong . . . um, Gwong-doong-wa?' (Do you speak Cantonese?) He looked at the man's pale blue eyes. He didn't. Mao twisted his face and glanced to the side wall for inspiration. 'You . . . have . . . to speak Cantonese . . . for –' He tried to think of the word, 'For this.' He gave the man an encouraging nod. Mr Mao said hopefully, 'Yes?' He simply wanted the man to go.

The eyes watched him. They unnerved him. They were a

94

European's eyes. They were like red hair and beards – they were something that made his Chineseness uncomfortable. They were –

The eyes went on gazing at him.

Mr Mao said, 'Gay daw ho?' On his desk was a wonderfully brocade-bound open book with hand-drawn Chinese characters on the pages. He tapped a page of characters with his fingertips. To a European they were totally and utterly incomprehensible. They turned a European, with his own civilization and all his learning behind him, into an illiterate. Mao, smiling slightly, said again, 'Gay daw ho?'

There was something in those eyes. They were not looking at him. Mr Mao, tensing a little, said – He changed his mind. Mr Mao said carefully in English, 'Do you have . . . a number?' He waited for the European to grin like some sort of moronic child, having won some sort of cheap victory, and start babbling back at him. Mr Mao said encouragingly, 'Yes?'

The Far Away Man sat facing him with no expression on his face.

Mr Mao said, 'Do you have a number?' Mr Mao said, 'A *number*!' Mr Mao, speaking English, said, 'You understand? Number? One, two' – he didn't know the word for three – '*Saam!*' Mr Mao, tapping at his pages of characters, said, 'Number? You understand? *Number?*'

The Far Away Man, his face unchanging, said softly, 'Hai.' He spoke Cantonese. The word meant 'Yes.' Mr Mao looked at him.

No, it was a fluke. By a fluke, he had simply made a noise that – Mr Mao said rapidly in Cantonese, 'You understand, do you, what method I use? I use the method which works by the addition of the numbers seven eight five?' He smiled thinly, 'You understand that, do you?'

'Hai.'

He still couldn't tell. Mr Mao, looking at him, tried to find the focus of his eyes. There was none. Mr Mao said –

The Far Away Man, sitting opposite him on the other side of the desk, was not there. His eyes were – Mr Mao said urgently in Cantonese, feeling the faintest pin pricks of adrenalin start in his wrists, 'You understand what I am, do you? I'm a fortune-teller. People come here to hear about their fortunes. Do you understand?'

The Far Away Man said, 'Hai.'

'*Do you understand what I'm saying to you in Chinese?!*'

The Far Away Man had no expression on his face. His future was set. There was nothing he did not know about its course already.

In the Future By Numerology room on the top floor of Cuttlefish Lane, The Far Away Man simply watched and waited.

3.52 p.m.

The Far Away Man said quietly, '. . . *Hai.*'

On the concourse of Kamikaze Mansions, Spencer, shouting above the chaos, yelled, 'Phil, I spoke to Christopher on the phone and he —' The hole in the centre of the concourse was making the concourse disappear. Into that, sledgehammer flying, the mad concourse digger was also disappearing. Spencer, dodging what looked like a shower of volcanic thunder eggs, disgorged from Etna at full blast, yelled —

Whatever he yelled was lost amid the sound and the fury. Spencer, cupping his hands over his mouth, bellowed —

Even bellows.

Auden yelled, 'See? Look! Do you see his dead body lying anywhere around here? No, you don't!' He swung the sledge-hammer like Thor and smashed at the end of a surviving flagstone on the edge of the hole. The flagstone, like Huckleberry Finn's raft hitting the rapids, slid over the edge and disappeared into the deep. Auden, leaping in after it and making sure of its demise by drowning it in torrents of falling sweat, swung the sledgehammer and put it out of its misery.

The hole was four feet deep: clay, granite lumps and the assorted effluvium of twenty-year-old garbage and rubble the builders used to reclaim the land. Auden, stomping on it with the hammer and shuffling his feet around in what in no way resembled the Mississippi mud, said, 'See? Sermons in bloody stones!' The look on Spencer's face disappointed him. Auden urged, 'Don't you see, he falls onto the same spot every time so if he fell onto the same spot he'd be –' His eyes glittered. Time for the big question. Auden said, '*Where?*'

Spencer said, 'Look, Phil, I've spoken to Christopher on the phone and I'm sure, with the right approach –'

Wrong! Dong! Next contestant. Auden yelled, 'Here! He'd be right here!' He saw something move – some small, wriggling inoffensive earth-fertilizing worm – and mashed it with his heel, 'He'd be where we can see him, which is –?' He waited. The seconds ticked away on the studio clock. Auden said, '*Well?*'

'Phil –'

'He has to be under the ground!' Auden said, 'Don't you see? A bird or a parachutist. Like them, he takes too long to fall. He takes thirty-storeys' worth of time to fall from a fourteen-storey building, so he isn't falling at all!' He tried to find some common ground between himself and the moron shaking his head at him, 'Don't you see, he hasn't got a calculator like you so he isn't timing it right.' The inoffensive worm was made of sterner stuff. It still wriggled. Auden smashed it with the sledgehammer. 'Don't you see, High-Dive Henry is under the ground! Who he is, in fact, is Low-Tunnel Terry!' Auden, his eyes shining, said with a quick glance over his left shoulder, 'Don't you see? They're all around. They're everywhere. They're here. Now. Under the ground.' For an awful moment Spencer thought he was going to say 'Keep watching the skies' – 'He's here, under us!' Auden said, 'Ha-ha!'

'*Why?*'

'What do you mean why?' On all the floors, in all the apartments the noise was going full blast. Auden yelled even louder, roared, 'What do you mean "*why*"?'

'I mean, why? I mean –' He ducked as Auden raised the sledgehammer and, cursing, gave the worm yet another death blow. Spencer said, 'Look at it scientifically, Phil, why is he under the ground?'

'For the same reason you thought he was up in the air!'

'I only thought he was up in the air because he couldn't have been anywhere else!'

'Exactly!' Auden said, 'Right! Exactly!' First prize. For a moment all the noise stopped in all the apartments and, from beneath the sledgehammer, under the worm mash, deep in the bowels of the earth, for a single brief instant, there was a dull, half-hearted thump.

Auden, raising the sledgehammer, said in triumph, 'Yeah!' as, almost as if to escape it, the ground beneath him opened up and, with a single shriek he disappeared totally down into it.

In the numerology office in Cuttlefish lane, The Far Away Man watched the little blue and white ribbons on the outlet grille of the air-conditioning unit as they blew and gyrated in the room and, whipping and flapping, touched each other and made little hissing noises. The ribbons had been turned over on the bars of the grille at their ends and made fast with staples: in the movement the staples glittered and flashed like little stars, like silver fish beneath a fast moving shallow river, like –

He heard them touching, tinkling as their ribbons ran like wakes behind sailing boats, as the loops over the bars rubbed and moved and wore down the paint on the grille and made it shine. Behind the grille there was a motor: it whirred ceaselessly, bringing in cool air, the ribbons all a-flying.

A-flying. It reminded him of something, of a children's book with big coloured cartoon drawings of cats and dogs and rabbits and strange, funny, happy, frightening things in forests with human faces on all the trees.

It reminded him of the smell of children after their baths in beds made of clean, new smelling sheets and the smell of talc and washed hair.

It reminded him.

The Far Away Man touched at his gun.

A-flying.

A-flying . . .

A-flying . . .

Once, in his life, his face had been alive, mobile.

Once . . .

Once, in his life . . .

What? What flew? What was a-flying? What, in all those books and in all those moments, went a-flying?

'*Why, your own shining hair, my dear. Why, your own happiness and laughter, my dear.*

'*And your laughter, my dear, goes flying straight to the clouds and makes the sun shine, and tears: why, my dear, they make clouds* . . .'

Why, my dear . . . Why, my dear . . .

For a moment, The Far Away Man closed his eyes.

Why, my dear . . . Why, my –

At his desk, rising, Mao said in Cantonese, 'Get out of my premises.'

The Far Away Man touched at the side of Mao's desk with his fingers.

'*Get the hell out of my premises. Now!* I don't know what you think you're playing at or who sent you, but I have a business to run and in exactly thirty seconds if you aren't gone I'm going to call the police and have you *thrown* out!'

A-flying. The ribbons all a-flying.

He felt . . .

The Far Away Man, in pain, said, 'No . . . !' He felt the taste of salt in his mouth. The Far Away Man said – He was looking away. For a moment Mao thought the man was going to be sick all over his desk. He was looking away, down at the floor, avoiding something. Mao looked. He was avoiding the sight of the air-conditioning, of the ribbons, of the –

Of the –

Of the –

The Far Away Man's face, looking down, grimaced with pain, fell into shadow and, with all his muscles turning to ice, Mao said suddenly in Cantonese, '*Oh, no!*' He knew him. He knew who he was. Mao, with his hands stiff on the top of his desk, his shoulders going back and all the colour going from his face in a single stiffening terror, said, 'Oh, no! I know who you are!'

He looked. The eyes came back. The eyes came back and they looked at Mao.

The eyes came back and they were no longer empty and they looked at him with death in them.

'No!' His body was stiff, paralysed. Mao, fighting to get his muscles working, said, 'Look, look, I've got it! Look!' His hands reached out for his desk and scrabbled at the papers and the ink tablets and brushes there. 'Look! *Look!*' He was speaking Cantonese. The eyes were staring at him. He could have been speaking Greek. The eyes were bright, shining. Mao said, 'No!' The brocade-bound book: he got his hand to the brocade-bound book and yanked at its binding. His fingers were not working. Mao said, 'Look! Look! I didn't know!' There was something inside the binding, something yellow — two sheets of yellow pages. Mao said, 'Oh, *please, please* –'

He felt –

It was gone.

He felt –

Gone forever.

A-flying, all, all . . .

. . . a-flying . . . All, all . . .

Mao, wrenching at the papers, yelled, 'Please! *Please!*' He tried to get up, but his legs gave way. Mao said, 'Please, I didn't know! I didn't *know*!' He saw the gun come up from nowhere and he said – The eyes were staring at him like suns and he could not remember one word of English! Mao, flailing his arms to keep his balance as his knees buckled under him, said in final, desperate, shrieked Cantonese, 'Mo! Mo-wah! MOWAH!'

A-flying. A-flying a-flying a-flying a-flying.

His eyes were full of tears.

He saw Mao's face.

He felt –

He felt nothing.

4.02 p.m.

The Far Away Man pulled the trigger.

In the Detectives' Room, O'Yee, shaking his head, said, 'No, it doesn't mean anything to me in English or Cantonese.' He looked hard at the yellow pages and the silver snuff box laid out in their glassene envelopes on Feiffer's desk, 'You're sure that's what Sharwood asked Wong to say – "knifeteeth"?' O'Yee, rubbing at his eyes where they still ran from the eye drops, said hesitantly, 'Could it be the brand name of something? A saw, or a –' He asked, 'Have you been onto Criminal Records in case it's an alias?'

'Yes.'

'And?'

'And it isn't.'

'And it isn't the brand name of something like a tool or –'

'Not so far as I can discover. I've been on to the biggest hardware supplier in the Colony and they can offer me "Knife Edge", "Knifesharp", and "Knifebright", respectively, a metal carpenter's rule, a brand of cleaver, and a range of stainless steel plates, but no "Knifeteeth".'

O'Yee said again, contemplating it, ' "Knifeteeth." ' he shook his head. He watched as Feiffer drew the two Chinese characters quickly and expertly on a scrap of paper and looked down at them.

They were just two characters.

Knifeteeth.

They meant nothing.

'Knifeteeth.'

In the oppressive heat of the Detectives' Room, with sweat running down his face and onto the desk where the yellow cholera pages and the snuff box were, Feiffer screwing up the scrap of paper and crushing it in his hand, said with sudden uncontrolled anger, 'Jesus Christ, Christopher, he's killed two people in the space of six hours! Surely to God there must be somebody somewhere who knows what it means!'

.38 S&W UMC

In the top floor office on Cuttlefish Lane, The Far Away Man, unloading the gun, glanced for a moment at the inscription on the back of the empty cartridge case.

.38 S&W UMC

It was the same on the live round he took from his pocket and fitted into the breech.

In his chair, Mao, with half his head shot away, was still briefly alive, and The Far Away Man, his eyes gone and distant, the sound of the ribbons on the grille of the air-conditioner only the faintest of impressions in his mind, placed the muzzle of his pistol carefully against the man's heart and, finally, finished him off.

Shen, Sharwood, Mao.

The two yellow pages torn from International Health Certificates were still sticking out of the torn brocade lining of the fortune-casting book.

The Far Away Man did not look at them.

They were of no further interest to him and, turning to go out, he left them, for anyone who might want them, exactly where they lay.

9

There were flies everywhere. In Cuttlefish Lane, they had come from nowhere and they circled around the doorway to the stairs to Mao's office and then, scenting blood, went up the stairs in droves.

In the street, Constable Sun said with his face still twisted in revulsion, 'That's what alerted me, sir. I was on patrol and I saw them swarming and I –' He forced himself to become professional, 'And upon entering the open premises on the first floor I discovered a male Chinese dead body which, on cursory examination, had suffered two bullet wounds: one to the heart and another to the right side of the head, removing part of the –' He swallowed hard, 'At approximately 16.25 hours I contacted the Station by telephone and –' He swallowed. Except for the flies, the street was deserted. Sun said, 'Whilst awaiting assistance I attempted to locate witnesses, but – um –' He brushed at the flies.

Feiffer said, 'But Cuttlefish Lane is the fish wholesaling area and by half past four everyone's gone home until the next catch comes in at 6 a.m.' It looked like a street in an end of the world movie. Feiffer, glancing at the uninformative sign on the side of the corridor entrance, asked, 'What was he, this man Mao?' The paint on the characters was flaking, making them difficult to read. 'It is Mao, is it?'

'It's Mao. I knew him. He was a numerologist who did the

103

fortunes of the fishermen and the wholesalers and, after they'd gone, private clients like ex-fishermen and sailors.' Sun, remembering looking at the face, said, 'Yes, it's him all right.' He looked at the flies and asked, a little green, 'Do you want me to go up there with you?' He saw Feiffer draw a deep breath in preparation for mounting the stairs and he thought for a moment the man had not heard him.

Sun, wiping at the sweat on his mouth and chin asked in a strained, anxious voice, 'Sir? Mr Feiffer? Do you want me to go up there with you?' He sounded urgent.

Sun said desperately, 'Sir, you don't want me to go up there again, do you?'

It was 4.48 p.m.

Feiffer shook his head.

The street was like an old end of the world movie.

In it, coming from everywhere in the thick, heavy heat, there were only the black, buzzing flies.

He had gone like a billiard ball down a side pocket. Spencer saw a light. The billiard ball had a box of matches with it and it was rolling along the slate table having an explore. On the rim of the hole, Spencer shouted, 'Phil? Are you all right down there?' The billiard ball had decided to smash up a bit of the mahogany table on its way. There were crashing sounds. Spencer shouted, 'Phil, answer me!'

There was a chuckling sound of a nature so diabolical it could have been coming, not from the hole, but from the Pit. Auden shouted back, 'Ow!' as his match went out. His shoes on what sounded like stone went clump, clump, clump. All the sounds in the apartments had stopped. The residents had come out on their verandas to see the show.

Spencer yelled, 'Phil!' He heard another 'Ow!' and then a scrape as Auden got another match going.

Spencer said, '*Phil!*'

Nothing. The billiard ball was evidently just rolling along, rolling along. Spencer demanded, '*Phil, what's down there?*'

It was an old coal bunker. For a moment, in the flame of a match, Spencer saw the black stains on the floor.

Spencer shrieked, 'Phil, what in the name of hell is down there?' He heard Auden shout a long way away, 'Hundreds! My God, hundreds!' He heard Auden shriek in extremis a long way off, 'My God, the place is full of them!'

Spencer, transfixed, said, 'Oh, God!'

'Thousands and thousands! Everywhere!' He heard Auden yell out in pain or joy, 'Aarghh!'

It wasn't Auden. It was High-Dive Henry.

There was a terrible thump, then snaps, then clickings, the sound of racks and bat-filled dungeon devices, cracks, snaps, metal tearing at metal.

Spencer said, 'No!'

The hole was dark, sinister, evil, the stuff of nightmares. Spencer, with one hand firmly on his shirt pocket to protect his new calculator from damage not covered by the twelve months' warranty – without a second thought – jumped feet first straight into it.

As usual, there was nothing. Macarthur had finished his work and gone downstairs to wait for the ambulance and, before the fingerprint and photographic teams arrived, in the room with Feiffer there was only Mao and the flies.

And the heat.

In the heat, the flies buzzed in swarms and forced their way under the rubber sheet covering Mao in the chair or, finding their way blocked, landed on the blood on the walls and floor and seemed to bathe in it.

Li Kit lai (6.3.59).

Chiang Shiao-yang (8.1.60).

The two yellow Health Certificate pages were the same as all the others, both made out in the same hand, and both without the name of the issuing office on the little circles of blue ink stamped on their margins. They were just like all the others.

They were nothing.

In the room, Feiffer, lighting a cigarette and trying to keep the flies out of his eyes with the smoke, flipped open the silk brocade-covered fortune casting book that had hidden them. It was old, in manuscript form, handwritten. He turned a page and glanced at the lines of characters written carefully in a fine hand that, when deciphered, would give a seeker after the future hope and certainty.

It was nothing. It needed a key to open it, a number. In the room, gazing at the flies as they fought to get at what had once been a living man, Feiffer said quietly in Chinese, 'Seven, eight, five.' The magic number. All the magic numbers and all the keys to the magic numbers were contained in Mao's head. Beneath the rubber sheet, the head was open and still seeping. There was nothing. The Far Away Man, so far in one day, had killed three times and there was no reason on Earth why, if he felt like it, he should not go on killing forever.

He had it all his own way. The desk and the doorknob in Mao's room, like the doorknob in the jade shop were running with moisture and there would be no fingerprints. And Cuttlefish Lane had been deserted and there would be no witnesses, and, even if there had been, in his anonymous grey suit with his anonymous face — with his unreal face — The Far Away Man would simply evaporate, disappear and cease to exist. In the room, as the flies wheeled in maddened circles at the rubber shroud, Feiffer said suddenly, 'You bastard, you do exist! People even claim to know you!' He went forward quickly and lashed at the flies and sent them buzzing harder, 'You lousy bastard, *who are you?*'

He was no one. He was nothing. U Ne: a Burmese; Koo Teh-cheung: Chinese, and Yen Pei chi, another Chinese; a Japanese: Harada, and now —

Li Kit lai (6.3.59)

Chiang Shiao-yang (8.1.60).

Two more Chinese. Their torn out cholera injection sheets all neatly, carefully and firmly made out in the same hand. Two more. It was hopeless. Feiffer, shaking his head, said softly, 'A shoe shine man, a naval officer, and now a Chinese fortune-teller — who the hell's next? The bloody Archbishop of Canterbury or the bloody President of The United States?'

And The Far Away Man, when Mao had obviously torn them from the brocade covered book to buy his life, had not even wanted the two yellow pages. He had not cared enough to take them with him. He had simply left them where they were and, if Macarthur was right, after Mao had taken the first killing wound in the head, had reloaded his single-shot gun and put a second bullet into the man's heart.

Mao's hand hung down from under the rough rubber sheet. There was blood on it. A single fly moved up it to try to break through the rubber to get to the main prize. Feiffer said, 'Seven, eight, five.' Magic. The future. There was no future. He turned the top yellow page over on the book, still gazing at the form beneath the rubber sheet and said softly, as almost a eulogy for a life based on its principles, 'Seven, eight . . .'

There was a number written on the back of the page.

The number, in characters, read I sap yat: twenty-one. Feiffer, looking down at the three Chinese characters scrawled hugely on the back of the first yellow page, said aloud, 'Twenty-one.' He turned the other page over. It was the same: twenty-one. It was a number. Someone's lucky number from which to tell a fortune. All you needed, apart from the barest knowledge of how the calculations were done, was the key casting book. It was on the desk in front of him. Feiffer, touching at it with his fingertips, said softly, 'Twenty-one.' They both had it, both Li and Chiang, both of the two Chinese named on the two Health Certificate pages. They could not both have it. Things didn't work that way. It was someone else's fortune, someone *connected* with them – someone who – Feiffer, flipping open the brocade book and running his eyes down the columns of hand written characters it contained with the flies forgotten in the room, said quickly, 'How does it work?'

Seven eight five.

It worked on seven eight five. First you took the lucky number and to it, you added the first number of the seven eight five – the seven: – giving . . . twenty-eight . . . and then you . . .

Feiffer opened the book to character number twenty-eight and found the numbered character.

The character read: 'Go'. It was in concert with a smaller character, a negative. The character read 'Go not'. The two characters in concert were marked with a pencilled cross. He looked back to the numbers on the back of the yellow pages and found two more crosses, written against the numbers faintly in pencil and almost erased by the folds.

He looked back to character number twenty-eight and the cross beside it. The cross against the characters in the brocade book and the crosses on the yellow sheets had been done with the same pencil.

There was equal pressure on them. They had been done by the same person.

Feiffer, clenching his fist, said softly, aloud, 'Think, think.'

He remembered.

And then, what you did for the second word or idea in the horoscope was take the lucky number again and, this time, add the second basic number – the eight – to it and then, looking it up . . .

Character twenty-nine, directly below, on the same page, was also marked with a cross.

The character read: 'told'.

Go not . . . told. In Chinese it would work out to mean 'Go not as told . . .' Feiffer said softly, 'Oh, my God . . .' It was happening, it was meaning something. It was somebody's fortune who at one time had had one of the yellow pages – both of them – and it was actually, finally meaning something!

And then, and then – the third number *five*. You added it to twenty-one and you got: 'Others'.

It was happening. It meant something. It meant: 'Go not as told by others.' It was the first line in the couplet the fortune would form.

Seven eight five. After that it was a matter of adding the two end numbers together and then, after that, the centre number and then the last and then . . . He moved quickly through the book to find the characters. They were crossed. All the characters for the fortune for the owner of the number twenty-one had been marked, crossed, made clear for the caster by little – Feiffer read aloud, 'Go not as told by others, But by other ways go.' There was at least one more step. It was like a haiku: first there was a statement and then a qualification and then, as the finale – as the point, the direction, the actual *future* – there was, there was always a single cryptic final line: the crux.

Feiffer, trying to think, standing in a dead man's room casting the fates for someone who might already be dead or never have lived, said urgently, 'First, the first number plus the lucky number, then the second basic number and then the third number, then the two end numbers and then the centre number and the last and then . . .'

Feiffer said, 'God! I've seen it done so many times!' His father had once even written a little monograph about it for the Shanghai Asian Society. He knew it. He had read it. He had seen it done. Feiffer said slowly, 'And then you – you subtract the two end numbers from the lucky number and then you add everything together for the last two characters!' He was right. He knew it. Feiffer calculating the numbers said, 'Characters number *six* and –'

And forty-one.

He turned the pages quickly and found the characters marked.

Six.

And forty-one.

In the vile, buzzing room, Feiffer read the complete couplet he had formed aloud. It read: '*Go not as told by others, / But by other ways go.*'

And the two last characters, in the brocade book, characters number six and forty-one: the last, final guiding line of the fortune – of the marked, crossed, vital fortune Mao had cast for someone whose number for some reason was twenty-one – those two characters, put together, read:

Knifeteeth.

In the terrible, fly-buzzing, bloody room, Feiffer, staring

down at the brocade-covered book and the two yellow pages on top of it said softly, '*Got you!*'

He hated it when Auden was having a good time. In the old underground coal bunker, Spencer vibrated like a tuning fork. It was pitch black. The voice sounded as if it was coming from Thor. The voice boomed, 'ALL THIS SCIENTIFIC STUFF IS OK IN ITS PLACE, BUT WHEN IT COMES TO IT YOU CAN'T BEAT THE OLD RELIABLE METHODS OF THE RUBBER HOSE AND THE SIZE THIRTEEN FIST IN THE FACE!'

It was Auden. He was somewhere in the black with a megaphone. Spencer, stumbling over something that made a metallic noise on the hard floor, said, 'Phil, are you all right? Where the hell are you?'

'I'M HERE, WHERE I SHOULD BE – ON THE GROUND, THINKING LIKE A COP!' The earth was shuddering with the decibels. Auden boomed, 'HOW HE DID IT, SEE, WAS HE PUT THE MEGAPHONE AGAINST THE BOTTOM OF A RAINPIPE THAT LEADS INTO A DRAIN JUST OVER HERE AND HE SHOUTED STRAIGHT UP LIKE THIS –'

Auden went, not, 'Aaaarrrggghhh!' but ... 'AAARRR-GGGGHHH!!!' The air hummed, it caught fire, it ripped in half. Bits and pieces of masonry and rubble fell down onto Spencer's head. Whatever it was on the floor rolled away making terrified tinkling noises. Auden thundered, 'AND THE SOUND WENT STRAIGHT UP THE RAINPIPE OUT OVER THE ROOF AND THAT'S WHY YOU COULDN'T TELL WHERE IT WAS COMING FROM!'

Spencer said indignantly, 'Who couldn't work it out?'

'YOU COULDN'T WORK IT OUT! HE WASN'T JUMPING FROM A FORTY-STOREY BUILDING OR WHATEVER YOU THOUGHT, WHAT HE WAS DOING WAS SHOVING THE MEGAPHONE UP AGAINST THE RAINPIPE EXIT, SCREAMING AT THE TOP OF HIS VOICE, AND THEN, WHEN EVERYONE IN THE APARTMENTS

TURNED UP THEIR VOLUME TO DROWN OUT THE NOISE –'

'*Will you stop shouting!*'

Auden, moderating his level a little so that not everybody in the civilized world would hear him, but only those domiciled in the Pacific or Indian Ocean areas, said, 'YOU'RE A REASONABLY AVERAGE GOOD COP, BUT THE TROUBLE IS THAT YOU DON'T SEE POLICE WORK PERSONALLY ENOUGH!' Auden informed the world, 'YOU TRUST PEOPLE. YOU THINK THEY COMMIT CRIMES FROM SOCIALLY DEPRIVED MOTIVATIONS, BUT THEY DON'T – THEY COMMIT CRIMES SO THEY CAN PUNISH BLOODY POLICEMEN!' Auden bellowed, 'BUT I GOT HIM. HE WAS TRYING TO ESCAPE THROUGH TO THE SEWERS, BUT I FOUGHT HIM IN SINGLE COMBAT IN THE DARK AND I SMASHED THE BASTARD OVER THE HEAD WITH THE LAST OUNCE OF MY STRENGTH AND LAID HIM LOW ON THE FIELD.' He wasn't having a good time. He was having a wonderful time. Auden bellowed with Churchillian triumph, 'THESE ARE NOT DARK DAYS, THESE ARE GREAT DAYS –'

No they were dark days. Spencer, for the first time in his life having an overwhelming urge to kill, yelled, 'Turn on the fucking light!' He took a step forward and knocked something over. He knew that sound. He had heard it once before in the basement of the Station. Spencer said, 'My God, guns. On the floor, there are –' Spencer said with his mouth hanging open swallowing darkness, 'My God, Phil, this is the testing range for –' He kicked. Something tinkled. He knew that sound. It was a bit of a –

Auden said, '*GUNS!* HE WAS TESTING HIS GUNS. THE TESTER MADE THE SCREAM THROUGH THE RAIN-PIPE SO PEOPLE WOULD TURN UP THEIR VOLUMES AND HE COULD TEST HIS GUNS AND MAKE THEM THINK THE THUMP WAS THE PHANTOM SUICIDER AT IT AGAIN!'

Auden howled, 'THE TESTING RANGE FOR ALL THE ILLEGAL GUNS IN THE ENTIRE COLONY – IN THE ENTIRE *WORLD*!' For an awful moment Spencer thought he was going to sing –

Auden exploded, 'AND I WAS THE ONE WHO FOUND IT!' From nowhere he lit a gas lantern with a hiss and a boomph and the entire coal bunker came bright with light. Auden, taking the megaphone away from his mouth, said happily, 'Ha-ha-ha-ha! I crashed down onto the bugger and he put up a hell of a fight – well, he would: he was a man who liked guns – A worthy enemy – But after a few good wallops over the nut with my Python he just gave up and –' He was hopping between the masses of guns and gun bits on the floor, picking his way between them with glee in a mad, ballistic game of hopscotch. Auden, looking as if he was going to wet his trousers any moment in unalloyed delight, said, 'Who's a clever boy, aye? Who's O'Yee going to grovel to just to say he knew? Aye? Who's –' There was a dark huddled mass between two piles of black pipe-like things that looked like home made versions of Uzi sub-machine-guns. Auden, picking the mass up with one hand, said, 'Bill, he fought like a devil. Well, he would. He was a gun man – you know, hardy and the rugged individual sort like me. But I –' He had the shapeless, unconscious thing in his hand. He lifted it up and gave it a consoling pat. Auden said, 'Aye? What do you think Special Branch is going to think of me *now*?' He dropped the unconscious body and it crashed onto the hard floor and almost bounced. Auden said, 'Tough, that's what you've got to be to survive in this man's world – tough and manly and uncompromisingly' – he searched for a word. It was all right. They were alone. Auden, patting himself on the chest – why not? everyone else was going to want to stand in line to say it – said, '*Macho!*'

He saw Spencer suddenly open his eyes wide and point to something and Auden said, 'Yes, it's the haul of the decade all right, the haul of the –'

Spencer was not pointing at him. He was pointing at something else.

Spencer said, 'Oh, no . . .' The clickings, the metal on metal, the – Spencer said, 'Oh, no!'

Spencer's eyes were staring.

Auden said, 'Well, I –' Auden said, 'Everybody's going to –' He looked down at the spot on the floor Spencer's trembling finger indicated.

It was a mass of gun parts.

Auden quivered. He retreated. He came forward. He retreated again. Auden, picking up the megaphone and thundering said reasonably, 'WELL, I HAD TO HAVE SOME SORT OF BLOODY REWARD, DIDN'T I?'

Auden, moving forward and stepping over the gun tester's discarded supine form, said with a catch in his throat, 'Bill, I'm only human.' For an awful moment he thought he was going to cry. Auden, leaning down even as he begged, his hands having a life of their own as they began stripping even more guns than the fourteen guns he had already stripped in the dark, said pleadingly, 'Bill, Bill, why can't O'Yee ever try to understand me the way you do?'

In the basement, Lim finished the last of the guns. He could understand someone liking them – when you came to it, they did have a certain mucky handed, male attraction.

Standing back in the ruined, smoky, shot-to-pieces little room and putting his hands on his hips to survey his handiwork, Lim said softly, 'Hmm.'

Odd things, weapons.

For some strange, unaccountable reason, they gave him an overwhelming urge to go home and beat up his wife.

In the Detectives' Room the phone rang. It was the Factotum. The Factotum, giving his name quickly, said urgently, 'I've seen him. I can see him now.' He paused for a moment, 'I'm in Hong Bay Road and I can see him across the street standing outside a factory.' The Factotum said, in case O'Yee was not clear, 'Him! The one who came into The Windjammer Club, I can –' The Factotum said urgently, 'He's turning. He's outside something called the Hong Bay Outboard Motor Company and he's –' The Factotum said, 'Get Mr Feiffer.'

O'Yee looked out quickly through the open door to the Uniformed section and the charge room. There was no one there. O'Yee said, 'Where are you now?'

'In Hong Bay Road! In –' The Factotum, lowering his voice for an instant so that O'Yee could hear the sounds of the street behind him said tightly, 'They fired me. They just gave me my cards and chucked me out and all they said –' He made a sniffing noise, 'I'm in a phone box just opposite the factory near the floating restaurant. I was just walking and trying to think and I –' The Factotum said, 'He's gone in!' If he hadn't been a hundred percent sure before he was now. The Factotum said, 'My God, I can see his gun!' He was babbling, 'My God, he turned and his coat came back and I –' The Factotum said, 'It's silver! I saw it glint in the sun!' The Factotum's voice was rising. The Factotum said, 'Quick, he's going in! He's – you'll miss him if you –'

'Stay there! I'm on the other line to –'

'*You'll miss him if you don't hurry!*'

O'Yee was already dialling the number for the fortune teller's on the other phone. He prayed Feiffer was still there. O'Yee said –

'He's gone in! You'll miss him! I'm going to have to –'

'Stay on the line!'

'I can't.' The Factotum, the voice going up again, said in protest, 'They fired me! It's my one chance to redeem myself!'

'You keep away from him and that's an order!' In the fortune teller's the phone was ringing and ringing. O'Yee, gripping the line to the Factotum in his fist, said to the ringing in the other phone, 'Come on . . . come on . . . !' O'Yee said desperately to the Factotum, 'Listen, listen . . .'

'He's gone in!'

'Stay where you are! Stay in the phone box, do you understand?' In the fortune teller's the phone was picked up and a voice – he recognized it as one of the technicians from Fingerprints – said, 'Yes?' and O'Yee said, 'This is Senior Detective

Inspector O'Yee. Get me Chief Inspector Feiffer immediately!'

'He's just going down the stairs to his car.'

The Factotum said, 'Oh, no!' O'Yee had no idea what he was referring to. O'Yee ordered the Technician, 'I don't care if he's going down the steps to the bloody nether world, get him!' He said fiercely to the Factotum, 'Stay there!'

The Factotum said, 'I know him!' He made a sort of sighing sound as if, suddenly, it all made sense. The Factotum, his one chance to redeem himself there in front of him for the taking, said incredulously, 'My God, I know him! *I actually know who he is!*'

O'Yee could see what was coming. O'Yee, throttling the phone to the fortune teller's in his other hand as the Fingerprint Man went down the stairs quickly to catch Feiffer, said with the sweat pouring off his face in the heavy atmosphere of the room, 'Don't you follow him in there! Do you hear me? You stay where you are! Don't you follow him in there!'

'*No?*' For a moment there was a sadness in the Factotum's voice, a resignation. The Factotum asked softly, '*No?*' Across the road The Far Away Man had gone into the factory. Maybe, in there, there was someone else like the Factotum, some other poor subservient retainer who had wasted his life in . . . The Factotum said again, '*No?*'

In the phone box in Hong Bay Road he smiled to himself.

Shaking his head as he put the phone down to go across the street and follow The Far Away Man into the factory, the Factotum said quietly to himself, 'Where else have I got to go?'

It was 5.21 p.m.

O'Yee shouted, 'Hullo! *Hullo!*

Squaring his shoulders, the Factotum touched at the Wing's eighty-five-cent corn-cob pipe in the pocket of his coat and, the traffic bothering him not at all, went slowly across the street into the factory with, he thought as he walked, for the first time in many years, a feeling of great and genuine dignity.

5.21 p.m.

In the Detectives' Room, O'Yee shouted down the line to a silent instrument that lay on the fortune teller's table as the

Fingerprint Man sprinted down the steps for Feiffer, 'Harry! Harry! For God's sake – *where the hell are you?*'

He knew the factory. He knew every inch of it. He had been there many times before and he knew every single part of it and every corridor and every room.

Inside the factory, in the dark, The Far Away Man turned right.

10

In the glass-fronted retail showroom at the front of the Hong Bay Outboard Motor Company, Feiffer said quickly, putting out his hand, 'It's all right.'

It wasn't all right. In the shop, a lone girl assistant, not a day over twenty, said in rapid Chinese, 'We've got a special Summer discount on three of our top horsepower models due to the cancellation of the final part of an export order to Australia.' She was moving away from Feiffer in the shop, backing towards the rear, touching at the brightly painted machines on display, tapping them, looking for somewhere behind their mechanisms to hide her hand. She stopped. Dressed in a light T-shirt advertising the motors and an almost transparent cotton mini skirt advertising the sex appeal that went with the ownership of one of the motors, she touched at her mouth. Maybe she was younger than twenty. Maybe she was too young to be working at all. The girl said desperately, as if to her mother, 'I'm only working here part-time because there was an export order cancelled – I didn't see anybody!' She saw Feiffer reach out to stop her moving and she moved away again, 'My father would kill me if he knew I was –' She looked down at her mini skirt and saw through it, herself, the outline of her panties, 'I don't know anything. I didn't see anyone!' She saw Constable Sun move quickly past the window on the street, his hand on his unbuttoned holster, 'I don't know anything! No one came in here! No one!'

'A European, an elderly man, maybe wearing a waistcoat and –'

'No!'

At the window, Sun shook his head. The Factotum had gone. Feiffer, cursing himself, said, 'A tall man with fair hair –'

'No.' The girl began backing away. She was not backing away from Feiffer. It was from the telephone on her desk. 'I was on the phone talking to my – to a customer and I –' The girl, nearing panic, said, 'If anyone had wanted to go into the factory they wouldn't have come through here anyway, they would have gone through one of the doors at the side!' It was the end of her job. The moment the police left she was going too – 'I've only got the job part-time to earn' – she looked down at herself again. From the window the uniformed Chinese policeman was also looking at her – 'to earn some money!' She looked at Feiffer. She was in tears, 'These are the clothes they gave me to wear! I didn't buy them!'

There were five other entrances to the factory, one to the main two-storey office area and at least four more around the side of the low, sprawling building where the assembly of the motors took place, and probably a loading bay as well. Feiffer said quietly, 'You haven't done anything wrong. All I want you to do now is just lock up and go home.'

'The factory's closed. Everyone's left. There's only me!' The girl said, 'I can't lock up. I haven't got the key!'

'Who has?'

'Mr –' The girl, moving further away from something, not, this time, her clothing or her father, said, 'Everyone's gone home, I'm just here in case a customer comes in off the street and inquires!'

'Someone went into the factory: the fair-haired man.'

'No. There's no one there!'

'Then who's got the key?'

'Mr –' She stopped. She began rocking. The girl, touching at her skirt and shaking her head, said, 'No one! There's no one! Honestly!'

'Who were you on the phone to?'

'No one! A customer!' The girl said, 'Mr Oliviera, my boss! Mr Oliviera!'

'In the factory?'

'*No!*'

Feiffer, still speaking in Chinese, said quietly, 'Is that why you got the job? Because of –'

'I'm twenty-two years old! My father wants me to finish university!' She looked again at Sun watching her from the window. Her father had never seen anything except a little girl. The girl said, 'I love him! We don't actually *do* anything!' No one understood. The girl, still moving backwards, said, 'Everybody wears short skirts these days!'

'What part of the factory is he in?'

'He's got the key. He has to stay on to –'

'All right.' Feiffer jerked his head to Sun and Sun looked away down the street. Feiffer said quickly, 'Listen, what you do is your own affair. All I want to know is –'

'There were two of them. I saw them from the side window. A fair-haired man and then, a little later, an older man: Europeans. I just thought –'

'OK.' Feiffer finally reached the girl and, laying his hand gently on her shoulder said, 'Is Mr Oliviera the only person still in the factory?'

The girl looked at him with wide eyes. She was not thinking. Ideas in her panic were only coming to her half formed. The girl said, 'Yes, of course! Of course he is. He's got the key!'

'Where is he now?' If he was alone in the factory he was the victim. If he was alone in the factory somewhere there was a door unlocked. Feiffer said quickly, 'Just tell me how to get to him!' He saw the girl's face tighten, 'I want to help him!'

'This is a –' She touched at an outboard, 'A – a Cutlass model 45E twin prop with –' She touched at her face.

Feiffer said, '*Please!*'

It was finished. Her job, university, everything. The girl,

turning the hand on the outboard motor into a fist of total resentment and frustration at, not Feiffer, but everyone, said with the light behind her picking up every curve and V of her woman's body under the dress, 'He's in the packing department! The third side door entrance! His name's Ernesto Oliviera! He's a Portuguese, from Macao! He's in the packing department working back!' She tried to make Feiffer understand, 'He's the boss of the whole factory: the director.' She looked down at her hands. They were clasped together in front of her like a little girl's.

The girl said sadly, 'He loves me. It's the only way we can meet.' She looked out through the window at Sun and then away again to the motors.

The girl, in floods of tears, begged suddenly, 'Please, he's the first man I've ever known. Please, please don't hurt him!'

Shen.

Sharwood.

Mao.

At the end of the darkened hangar-like assembly floor of the factory The Far Away Man could hear movement. It was coming from a long way in front of him, from behind a darkened, closed door that led into the packing room.

Shen.

Sharwood.

Mao.

The Far Away Man touched at a spot of blood on his mouth with the corner of his handkerchief.

Oliviera.

The Far Away Man went forward.

There was nobody else in the Station. Lim had obviously gone off duty or, still on duty, had gone off somewhere to buy a gun book, and all the other Chinese Constables were either out on their beats or between shifts. The Station was empty. There was no one else there except him.

At his desk, O'Yee, trying to work out how to contact

Auden and Spencer, ran his hand through his hair and said, 'Shit!'

There was no way to contact Auden and Spencer. O'Yee said, 'Shit!'

5.32 p.m.

There was no one.

O'Yee said, 'Shit! Shit! Shit!'

His gun was lying in the open top drawer of his desk, black, menacing and lethal. For all the good it was going to do to help Feiffer and Sun it could as well have been a licorice flavoured lollipop.

There was no one.

In the Detectives' Room, moving, pacing, finding nowhere to settle, O'Yee said, 'Shit! Shit! Shit!'

O'Yee said hopelessly, '*Goddamnit!*'

At the third side entrance to the factory the sun was beating down and turning the tarmacadam to liquid. The door was unlocked. Feiffer, trying it, said softly to Sun, a foot behind him, 'Listen, you know this character's description: tall, fair-haired, European, probably wearing a grey suit. And armed. Understand?' He looked at the Savage 77 pump action combat shotgun cradled in Sun's hands. 'You stay out here at this door and if I miss him or he takes me out –' The shotgun was loaded with five 12 gauge SG cartridges, each one charged with nine lead buckshot rounds of .33 calibre. 'Then you bloody well take him out – all right? Understand? No warnings, no arguments, no nothing. If you see him, shoot him.'

Already in the course of less than nine hours, The Far Away Man had killed three people. He had a single-shot pistol. It was all he needed.

Feiffer, shaking a little in spite of the overwhelming heat, said clearly and firmly, 'And whatever you do, don't fucking *miss*!' He saw Sun's face. For an instant, he thought he should say something.

There was nothing to say.

5.33 p.m.

Drawing his gun and pulling at the oiled silent door in a single movement, Feiffer, his mouth dry and parched, his breath coming in short, painful stabs, went quickly at a crouch into the enveloping darkness of the factory.

'*I can hear you, you bastard.*' The Factotum was in the factory on the far left of the unpainted wooden door. He listened. He could hear him. The Factotum cocking his head, said softly to himself, '*I can hear you moving.*' He touched something by his hand. It was metal. '*I can hear you on the cement floor walking on the balls of your feet.*' He heard a faint swishing noise, '*I can hear your coat touching things. I can hear you.*'

He was in there. He was like all the others. He was the same and he knew how they moved, how they walked, how they carried themselves: he had heard them walk across his lobby – he had seen them, studied them. He knew them. There was something about them. Peering into the gloom the Factotum picked out rows of half assembled motors in silhouette. There was an aisle between them. He would go down there. Gentlemen always went by the direct route. Getting up a little, he strained his eyes and saw in the faint light coming from covered up windows, almost – it amazed him – almost the luminous footprints where the man had gone.

It didn't amaze him. No, not after so many years. There was a smell, a look, a feel to people like him. He had known them all his life the way a hunter knew an animal. There were no luminous footprints – he simply knew.

He *knew* where the man would go.

He knew everything about people like him.

Everything about all of them.

Every last one of them.

There was something about them, a look, a –

The Factotum, rising, said softly, '*I'm your chronicler, your Boswell. There's nothing I don't know about people like you.*' The Factotum said louder than he had intended, 'Want a little joke on your way to the bar? George has got one for you.'

He heard a sound and he stiffened. The Factotum said softly,

'*I know you've stopped. I heard you.*' He was unafraid. On his haunches, the Factotum smiled to himself. The Factotum said, '*I hear you. I hear and obey. I know all the gentlemen's wishes before they even know them themselves.*' The Factotum said softly, '*Want a whisky and soda? Here I am with it on a silver tray before you've even thought about it.*' The Factotum said in a hiss, 'Oh, thank you, George. Good old George. Well done, George. – Thank *you*, sir.' The Factotum, moving quietly, said in a whisper, '*I know who you are and for once in your life you're going to do something for me and get my job back.*' He reached the far end of the aisle and, squatting down, touched at the floor with the palm of his hand. It was, as he knew, concrete. It was cold and a little moist. The Factotum, smiling to himself, said softly, '*And then I'm going to do what I should have done years ago: I'm going to take the Club for every penny it's got and look after myself for a while.*' The Factotum, blinking back tears, said softly, '*And then I think I might marry and get someone to look after me for a change.*'

The Factotum said, '*You've stopped.*'

The Factotum said, '*Do you know I'm here?*'

There was a movement.

The Factotum said, '*For the first time in your life are you wondering?*' He listened. The factory floor was still, '*For the first time in your life have you got a doubt? Are you confused?*' He listened. He heard a hesitant noise as if someone – The Factotum standing up, peering hard into the failing half light, said vehemently, happily, '*Don't tell me you're frightened of old harmless George?*' His voice was nothing but the faint sound of breathing. He had to fight to keep it down. The Factotum said with his mouth hard and set as he moved, '*Don't tell me, for all your 'airs and graces and confidence, don't tell me that somebody has finally, at last, seen right through you and knows –*' The Factotum had to fight to keep his voice down. It was his triumph, his victory.

The Factotum, moving forward along the darkened aisle, said to himself so softly that there was no sound and the words were all in his mind, 'Don't tell me, Mr Club Member, that somebody, finally, after all those years, knows exactly what you *are* —'

The Factotum, smiling to himself, moving forward, shaking his head, said quietly, 'No, don't tell me that's happened at last.' The Factotum said with hatred, 'Goodness me, George, I say: *where would we all be then*?'

There was no key. In the outboard shop, at the door, the girl put her fist to her mouth.

There was no key.

The phone was dead. After he had spoken to her from the factory, Ernesto had cut it off to work back until she had finished at ten.

The street was full of people and there was no key. She looked back at the outboards.

They were valuable, in her trust.

Wearing that stupid skirt, looking like some sort of little Suzie Wong doll, the girl, staring fixedly down at the unlocked and unlockable glass front door said in Chinese, 'I'm twenty-two years old! I've got a right to do what I want with my life!'

There were no customers. There never were any customers. Customers didn't talk to girls in mini skirts. Customers talked to someone who could offer them a real discount or discuss the merits of mechanisms and performances with them. Customers —

In the strong summer light, she knew people could see right through her skirt and right through her T-shirt.

She had no key to the door.

She could hold it back no longer. She was twenty-two years old.

At the door, with her hand covering her face, the girl in the mini skirt clenched her fists together and wept.

His eyes had adjusted. It made no difference. There were only shadows, silhouettes. All the windows had metal security shutters up on them and there was no light. He heard a noise, a sound, but it was nothing, only a swishing. Whispers. He heard whispers, movement, a sort of talking, muttering, whispering –

Nothing.

For an instant he thought he saw a light, but it was nothing more than a movement, again, a shadow, a dullness for an instant on a far wall.

There was *nothing*.

The Factotum was inside, somewhere, moving around.

He listened hard for the man's shoes on the ground.

There was only a rustling. Feiffer, moving a little forward, said softly, 'George . . .' What the hell was the man's last name?

He thought for a moment he heard something creak: a piece of wood, leather on cement, the roof maybe cracking in the heat.

Nothing.

In the inky blackness, there was only a silent, inky blackness.

Feiffer, moving forward, crouching, his gun out in front of him searching the darkness like a torch, said urgently, '*George* –'

He had him.

He was ahead, moving, and he had him.

He saw him.

He saw his shadow and it was him.

In the centre aisle, the Factotum ran his tongue across his lips and felt his breath catch.

It was him.

He heard someone call his name and he stopped.

The door opened. He saw the light go from his office like water, spilling out onto the central aisle. Oliviera, in the corner of the packing office, said in a gasp, 'No –!' He knew who it was. It had been in the papers.

He knew who it was. Oliviera, grasping the room's sole weapon – an unpacking hatchet – backing against the corner of the room, said in extremis, 'No –! No –!' He had the envelope the man wanted in his other hand. He had it outstretched. Oliviera said, 'Look –! Look –!' He saw The Far Away Man in the doorway: a silhouette, a shadow, a nemesis. Oliviera said, 'You can have it! You can have it all!' The hatchet was lowering his hand of its own accord. He was losing the strength to keep it up. Oliviera said, 'Please –!' The envelope was out, being offered in his outstretched hand. He felt his bowels turn over and he thought any moment his sphincter muscle was going to go. Oliviera said, 'Please . . . *take it!*'

He saw The Far Away Man come in and close the door behind him. There was only a little desk lamp illuminating the packing office, casting only a circle of light around the desk and he could not see The Far Away Man's face. Oliviera, shuddering against the wall, said, 'I read it in the papers! I know!' He pushed the envelope out even further. Oliviera, lapsing subconsciously into Portuguese, said, 'Please! It's all over! It wasn't anyone's fault! It just happened that way!' He realized what he was doing. He saw the gun. Oliviera said in English – Oliviera said in Portuguese – everything was wrong – 'Mother of God, you're not –'

Oliviera said, with the hatchet coming back up again in his hand, '*Who are you?*'

He had him. He had him. He had him. Fifteen yards from the door to the packing office, the Factotum said in a whisper, 'Got you!'

He had him.

The Factotum, moving quickly in the dark felt tears of triumph on his cheeks. He felt their salt at the sides of his mouth.

The Factotum, his mouth drawn back in a fierce, triumphant grin, moving to the door, said aloud, 'Found you! You lousy, bloody bastard – *I've found you!*'

Voices. Sounds. Whispers. Shadows. Movement. There was a central aisle in the assembly area that led to – that led to the sounds and the voices and the shadows.

Feiffer, moving, called out, 'George –'
He heard a whisper, a sound, a flurry of movement.
Feiffer called out, 'George!'

Oliviera, feeling his strength coming back, shaking his head,
said, 'No, oh no. I don't know who you are, but oh, no –'
He saw the man touch at the sample packing case for the
second cancelled export shipment of the Cutlass Model 45E
motors to Australia. He saw the long fingers touch at the
documentation slips taped to the side. The slips had the word
AUSTRALIA printed on them in red Roman letters. But they
were no good to him. They were wrong. Oliviera had the main
brown envelope from the case in his hand. Oliviera, lifting up
the razor-sharp hatchet, said, 'Oh no. No, you don't. I know
what this is and I'm not falling for it.' He saw the gun in The
Far Away Man's hand. It was silver, glittering. It was a child's
toy. Oliviera, moving forward with the hatchet out in front of
him, grinning, said, 'No, I didn't come this far to fall for some
sort of cop trick like this one!' The man was still out of the
circle of light from the desk lamp. He looked at the gun. It was
a toy. It was a trick. Oliviera said, 'Turn around!' He heard a
noise from outside in the assembly room and knew it was all a
trick. Shen. Sharwood. Mao. All on the radio. All lies. All a
police trick. Oliviera, moving away from the wall and facing
the shadow of the man at the packing case, said, 'Turn around
you bastard and admit it's a trick or I'll slice your fucking guts
out and claim you were a fucking burglar!' Oliviera shouted,
'Turn around!'
The Far Away Man turned into the light.
It was happening in a dream, a nightmare. It was happening
in slow motion.
In the light, The Far Away Man looked at him.
Clearly, in the circle of light, Oliviera saw his face.
It was a dream, a nightmare.
Again.
In the dream, as his heart stopped, Oliviera saw him turn.
Into the light.

He saw his face.

Over and over and over and over . . . It was happening over and over and over and over . . . Oliviera said— There were no words. He was mute in the dream, defenceless, a spectator.

The Far Away Man turned into the light.

He saw his face.

Oliviera said —

He saw the gun. Real. Black. He saw the black muzzle of the silver gun yawning at him, swallowing him up.

He saw The Far Away Man turn.

He saw his face.

Oliviera said, 'NO!!'

He was jammed, stuck, caught in the cogs of a nightmare, going round and round.

He saw the gun.

He saw the man turn into the —

He heard. He saw —

A thump. He felt a thump. In his dream he felt —

He heard a word. In his dream, he thought he heard a word. He thought, for an awful moment, a coffin had opened up and the thing inside had opened his mouth and said a word.

He heard it. It was his own name.

'Oliviera.'

He looked down and all his chest was blown away, falling like —

He thought he screamed. He thought he opened his mouth and then in his dream —

And then the roar and the flash of the gun, tearing his chest to shreds in the packing room moments after it had torn his chest to shreds in his dream, threw him against the back wall and, with the envelope and the hatchet still out in his offering hands like surrender weapons, enveloped, consumed utterly, he slid down onto the floor and died.

'YOU BLOODY BASTARD!'

In the shop at the front of the traffic, the girl in the mini skirt actually heard the shout above the traffic in the street.

They were killing him.

She heard the shot as it went echoing and echoing inside the walls of the factory.

The girl in the mini skirt, releasing her hold on the unlockable door shouted, 'No!'

It was Ernesto.

They were killing him.

He was all she had. She was twenty-two years old and Oliviera was all she had.

With her skirt flying up behind her in the dying light of the day, not caring if anyone saw or what they thought, the girl began running to the side of the building to help.

In the Detectives' Room, O'Yee shouted on the phone, 'I've got to have some back-up, do you understand? And I need it now!' O'Yee said, 'I need at least four men!' He shouted down the line to the North Point Station Officer, 'Goddamnit, no! Half an hour won't do! I need them *now*!'

He glanced at the wall clock.

5.43 p.m.

O'Yee, sweat pouring off his forehead down his face onto the mouthpiece of the phone, said desperately, 'For God's sake! You must have someone —!'

In the open door to the office the Factotum was hanging onto The Far Away Man like a monkey. In the aisle, with both the Factotum and The Far Away Man clearly outlined in the open door, Feiffer shouted, 'George! Get away from him!' He had his revolver out in both hands, the hammer back and cocked, weaving the weapon to get a clean shot in. 'Let him go! Get away from him!' The Factotum, hanging on, was grunting and pulling at the man. The Far Away Man was staggering into the office with him on his neck and back. 'For Christ's sake let him go so I can get a shot in!' He saw The Far Away Man reach down and get something in his hand, something from somewhere in the office, a weapon, a —

It was an unpacking hatchet. He was turning, twisting, trying to use it. Feiffer yelled, 'George —!'

'YOU BLOODY BASTARD!' The Factotum, hanging on, was literally shouting in the man's ear. He had The Far Away Man's head in his crooked elbow and he was pulling, wrenching. The Factotum yelled, 'You owe me! For all the years — *you owe me*!' The Far Away Man had the hatchet up and at his face level. The Factotum, wrenching at the man's hair, yelled, 'You're going to tell them! You're going to tell them why I knew you and why I let you in!' He was pummelling at the man's head and pulling at his hair and face. The Factotum, trying to kick as The Far Away Man lifted him off the ground, yelled —

The Factotum was in the way. He was covering him, blocking him, masking him. Feiffer, taking a single step forward to get him in killing range, ordered the man, 'Turn him around! If you can't get loose of him turn him around so I can —' He saw, in a single, unbelievable moment, the Factotum wrench at the man's head, and then, in his hand like a scalp, he had half the man's hair. Feiffer, lowering the gun, said, 'Oh my God . . .'

He had it in his hand. It had come away. It was his hair. It had come away cleanly, easily. Under the hair, the scalp was pink and smooth, like a — The Factotum, loosening his hold, said in horror, 'Oh my God . . .' He fell back onto the floor. The Factotum, facing him, still masking the man from Feiffer said almost conversationally, 'Oh, my God, you're —' His mouth was open in disbelief. He saw The Far Away Man's eyes turn to him. The eyes were pale and dead, nothing. They were not there. The Factotum, touching his hands to his face, said in horror, 'My God, I remember!' The Factotum said, 'Sir, I —' He seemed to jump as something touched him on the neck and he began to turn, staring at Feiffer. The Factotum opened his mouth to say something and in that awful instant Feiffer saw The Far Away Man's face and knew him.

He knew who he was.

He knew him.

The Factotum began to come towards him and Feiffer, lowering the gun, knew him. He knew his name. He knew who he was. Feiffer, about to say his name, said — He saw the Factotum take an unsteady step towards him.

Feiffer said —

In the driveway, Sun yelled, 'No!' He had the riot gun up and ready. He saw the girl coming towards it with her skirt and hair flying.

Sun, hearing the shouts and the shot from behind the closed door of the factory yelled out to her, 'No! Get away!' She was going towards the first side door. Sun, dropping the riot gun to run forward to catch her, yelled at the top of his voice, 'No!'

He knew him. He knew who he was. And in that awful instant, the Factotum's neck where it had been severed by the hatchet came cleanly away and as the Factotum collapsed virtually into his arms with his mouth still open to make an apology for something he had done, or for his entire life, Feiffer was overwhelmed in a single, violently gushing fountain of spraying blood.

Six-oh-eight p.m., exactly.

In the dully lit packing office Feiffer looked down at the contents of the envelope held spread out in Oliviera's hand.

L. P. Kim (2.3.44)

Tang Tsek-ming (19.7.49).

Two single yellow pages torn from two yellow International Health Certificate books.

In the office, there was only the single, dull illumination from the desk lamp.

Outside, in the real world, it was near dusk.

Outside, it was the last hour of the day.

In the office, in the circle of light from the overturned desk lamp, Feiffer waited silently for the night.

11

'How the hell did he get past?'

On the phone, Feiffer snapped back at the Commander, 'He got past because this is bloody Hong Kong, not the bloody Abu Wadi Oasis with two dogs and a camel!' He was at home, showered, his face etched with fatigue, 'He got past because at the exact bloody moment he chose to make his bloody exit that damned girl charged around the side of the factory in hysterics and Sun's first duty was to get her out of the line of fire!' It was not Sun's fault. He had done the only thing. Feiffer, rubbing at his face, said, 'What the hell should he have done? Cut her in half with the bloody riot gun just so he could get a goddamned shot in at The Far Away Man to make me happy? He did the right thing!' He had. It was indisputable. Feiffer said, 'It wasn't his fault. I would have done the same. I did do the same! All I needed to have done inside the factory was blow the Factotum away and I could have slaughtered The Far Away Man where he stood, but I didn't, and neither did Sun – and maybe that's the difference between him and us!' A long shower in his apartment had washed away only the blood. Feiffer said reasonably, 'Neal, it was just bad luck!'

'Then there's a hell of a lot of it around!' The Commander was not to be mollified. The Commander said, 'And now you tell me you know him!'

There was a silence.

'Well, do you tell me that?' The Commander was also at home. By the tone of his voice his family was also out and his apartment was also empty and silent. The Commander said, 'Well, if you do, then who the hell is he?'

'I don't know who he is! I just —' Feiffer said irritably, 'I — He looked familiar! I thought I knew him once, but I — but I can't place him!'

'Neither could the Factotum at that bloody Club!'

'No!'

'And he's bloody dead!' The Commander said, 'And so is a shoe shine man, and a naval officer, and a bloody fortune teller and so is —' The Commander demanded, 'Oliviera, do you at least know who he was?'

'He was what he seemed to be!'

'He *seems* to be a corpse!'

The shower had done no good. Feiffer, with perspiration standing out on his face, said tightly, 'He was the owner and managing director of the Hong Bay Outboard Motor Company. About a year ago they won a big export order of motors to Australia and they tooled up to meet it, then about five months ago, the Australians realized that the tender he had put in from America was in fact going to be filled from Hong Kong so they cancelled it and sent him and his company straight down the road to instant bankruptcy. Since then, according to his girlfriend in the shop, Oliviera has been working back every night in the export department trying to stave off bankruptcy by finding a new market.'

He got in before the Commander could ask, 'He's been living on a week by week basis at a local hotel. I had a forensic team turn it over and what they got was nothing.' He could hear the Commander breathing. Feiffer said, 'And what I got — apart from two dead bodies and a bath in blood — were two more yellow pages, namely L. P. Kim (2.3.44) and Tang Tsek-ming (19.7.49).'

He could almost hear the Commander totting it all up. Feiffer said, 'So that's a grand total of five Chinese, one Burmese, one Japanese and one Korean — *all right*?' The apartment was empty and silent and, at the phone, Feiffer wished his wife and son might come home to fill it with their voices, 'And in my full report, delivered to you in the morning, it'll go on record that as far as I'm concerned PC Sun did exactly, to the letter, the only thing he could have done, and I'm sorry if I couldn't extricate myself from a near bloody headless man to shoot the bastard myself, but that's the way it was!' The sweat was pouring down his face and getting into his collar. Feiffer, gasping with the effort, said, 'OK? *Is that all right with you?*'

'And you say the Factotum knew him too.'

'I didn't say that! O'Yee said he said that on the phone!' Feiffer, at the end of his patience, said, shaking, 'Look –'

'If you knew him and the bloody Factotum knew him, then how come nobody can put a name to him? The description's clear enough: he's six foot, fair-haired –'

'Half his bloody fair hair came out in the Factotum's hand!'

'I don't care if half his bloody head came away! How many bloody people are there in this colony with a description like that?'

'Thousands!'

'That you know personally?'

'I don't know him personally! I just –' What? Feiffer said, 'I just –'

'What? *Recognized* him?'

'If I'd recognized him I'd know who the hell he was!'

'Then who the hell is he?'

'I don't know! I didn't believe the bloody Factotum when he said he knew him either without knowing his name, but, obviously, like me, he bloody must have!' Feiffer said, 'I don't know. In the factory, for an instant, it was almost as if he –' It was hopeless. There was no answer. Feiffer said, 'I don't know. All I know is that, suddenly, for no apparent reason, the Factotum stood back and – and got almost apologetic, as if –' He saw it happen again. 'I don't know! It was almost as if –' Feiffer said, 'Neal, the truth is that I know him, but I haven't the faintest idea who he is!'

'You do know that if he keeps the killing up at this rate –'

'Yes!'

'Or if he suddenly stops –'

Feiffer said softly, 'Yes.'

'– then we'll never get him, Harry, never.'

Feiffer's hands were still trembling. There was an ashtray on the telephone table in front of him and he reached inside his coat for a cigarette and lit it. Feiffer said quietly, 'Yes I know that.'

The Commander's voice said quietly, 'Harry, I spoke to the Commissioner before I came home and gave him what I had: the list of the dead and the list of the yellow pages and – and "knifeteeth" – and –' There was a pause. The Commander asked, 'Are you listening?'

'Yes.'

'And then he asked me one question, Harry, just one. About witnesses – And I told him there was a total of three: the jade shop owner, Mui; George, the Factotum at the Windjammer Club, and –'

Feiffer said quietly, 'And me.'

'And you.' The Commander said, 'And Mui in the jade shop said he didn't know The Far Away Man.'

'And the Factotum did.'

The Commander said, 'Harry, I have to ask: is he someone you know?'

'No, he isn't someone I know!'

'You said you recognized him for Christ's sake!'

'I said I –' Feiffer said, 'I did! I did recognize him but I don't know who he is!' Feiffer said, 'Whoever he is, he's changed!'

'In what way?'

'I don't know in what way!'

'Harry, I've known you for a long time –'

Feiffer said again, 'I don't know him!'

'If he's a friend –'

'*I don't know him!*'

'You said you did!'

'I don't know him *now*!'

'Why not?'

'I don't know why not, but I don't!' "Knifeteeth," yellow pages, naval officers, shoe shine men, fortune tellers, silver snuff boxes, outboard motors: it was all impossible, insane. Feiffer said, 'Neal, just for a moment, I thought I – but I simply don't know who he is!'

'Sun said in his report to Internal Affairs that you ordered him to shoot first.'

'We didn't have any back-up. I ordered him to shoot first because it seemed the only reasonable tactic to adopt.'

'Before or after you thought you knew who he'd be shooting at?'

Feiffer said, 'Before.'

'And after?'

He could see what was coming. Feiffer said evenly, 'I stand by my comment that Sun did the right thing getting the girl away. Whatever my personal feelings might have been, he did the right thing in –'

'*Harry, did you hold off shooting that bastard in the factory because you knew him or not?*'

'I was covered in blood! I couldn't have seen to shoot at the fucking moon, let alone a man!'

'You weren't covered in blood when the Factotum attacked him!'

'Well I'm only sorry I didn't realize that at the time or I would have killed the Factotum before he got in the bloody way! That would have simplified the situation enormously! And, come to think of it, since I should have also known in advance that the girl was going to come around and screw up Sun's line of fire, I'm sorry I didn't kill her too when I had the chance in the shop! And why not Sun as well? That way, I could have stood out in the driveway myself and not had to worry about him having to save her because he would have been dead and so would she!' Feiffer, losing control, said bitterly, 'And how about the shoe shine man and Sharwood and the fortune teller and Oliviera himself?' Feiffer said,

'Christ Almighty, Neal, I've cracked the secret of good city policing in one – all you have to do is kill every citizen at birth and then, by God, at last, you're left with the perfect –'

'I'm only quoting what the Commissioner said!'

'And I'm quoting to you what bloody happened!' Feiffer said, 'Goddamnit, Neal, I've got to go back to the Station in ten minutes to go over everything I've already been over twenty times – do I really have to put up with this shit as well?'

'Do you or do you not know who The Far Away Man is?'

'Yes!' Feiffer said, 'Yes! He's someone I know! He's someone I knew! He's someone who –' Feiffer said, 'He's changed! I can't put a name to him! He's –' Feiffer said desperately, 'I don't know, Neal, I swear to you, just like everybody else in this case, I just don't know.'

It was 8 p.m.

Outside, in the city, it was night.

Feiffer, on the phone in the empty apartment, said softly, 'I don't know. I just don't know.'

Some dark Presence watching by my bed,
The awful image of a nameless dread –

In the apartment, on the phone, Feiffer said softly, 'I don't know. Neal, I swear to God – I just don't know . . .'

On the veranda of his fourth-floor apartment on Beach Road, The Far Away Man awoke and all the lights of the harbour and the ships winked out and blurred in his eyes like stars. He had fallen asleep in a cane chair with his head on his hand: in the lights from the harbour he took his hand away and saw no perspiration on his palm.

He ran his palm across his temple and little curling hairs were there between his fingers. He touched at his thinning hair and brought the hair away in clumps.

He touched at his scalp. In the heat it was cold and smooth. The lights from the harbour, from ships and floating restaurants, from sampans and junks going out to the fishing grounds, moved in front of his eyes like coloured beads.

He leaned a little forward and below the railing of the veranda he could see the lights of all the shops and cars along the waterfront and, here and there, flickering in a haze of smoke, the kerosene lanterns of the cooked food stalls and night sellers.

Hong Kong.

It seemed, sometimes, he had never really known anywhere else. On his lap, sliding a little as he slumped in the cane chair, was the gun box. He touched at it and felt the warmth of its wood on his hand.

Shen.

Sharwood.

Mao.

Oliviera.

It seemed, sometimes, in Hong Kong, he had never known anything else. The joints in his knees hurt and he drew his legs back a little and moved the gun box to a firmer spot on his lap. The lights were all blurred and coloured, some of them moving out to sea.

It seemed he had never known anything else.

The Far Away Man thought he made a sound, but there was no sound. He thought of coloured ribbons flying in the wind.

The lights blurred. He shook his head and wondered what the ribbons were. For another moment, he thought he slept. He saw . . . He saw sand, and an old wooden bridge over sand. He touched at the gun box.

He saw sand and streets and hills and –

He tried to think what the ribbons were.

The gun box was hard and warm in his hands. Gripping it, The Far Away Man said, 'Shen! Sharwood! Mao! Oliviera!' Sand. Bridge. A wooden bridge going across sand and a bright blue harbour, and boats – he saw boats and barges, tug boats. He heard . . .

He heard the popping of tug boats as they flurried across the blue harbour beneath the bridge. He saw the lights of Hong Kong. Not this harbour, another, a long time ago. He saw –

Shen. Marwood. Mao. Oliviera.

No, none of them.

The Far Away Man said, '*Wait!*'

No sound came out.

The Far Away Man, running across the wooden bridge and feeling the splinters in his bare feet – tough, hardened, sand-calloused bare feet – said, 'Wait! *Wait!*'

There was no sound.

He remembered.

The Far Away Man said, 'Wait . . . !'

On the bridge, in his bare feet, far away from . . .

The Far Away Man said urgently, 'Wait! *Wait!*' The lights blurred and there was a hard, twisting pain in his guts and he called out in pain.

There was no sound. He did not move.

He remembered. He was young, a child. He saw . . .

On the bridge, The Far Away Man said, 'Hey! Wait!' There was a barge carrying an old propeller driven aeroplane on its deck, working its way slowly under the bridge and The Far Away Man called out, 'Look! It's a *Mustang!*'

Long ago. Far away.

Not here.

With –

The Far Away Man said, 'Look! It's a Mustang!' He knew all the names of all the aircraft in the war. The Far Away Man called out to his friend, 'Look! It's an American Mustang!'

On the bridge, his friend paused. His friend, his mouth open, looking down, said –

The Far Away Man's eyes were full of tears.

The Far Away Man said, 'Wait, please wait . . .' Hot. It was hot on the bridge and his friend, like him, wore no shoes, and his feet, like his, were calloused with youth and sand.

Shen. Sharwood. Mao. Oliviera.

The Far Away Man said to his childhood friend, 'Wait . . . !' His friend looked at him.

In Hong Kong, all the lights blinked and blurred in his eyes.

The Far Away Man said, 'Australia. We're in Australia. In Australia . . .' He was the expert. He knew all about it. He even knew how to make whistles from the leaves of trees and how some spiders . . .

The Far Away Man, on his veranda, touched at his gun box and felt its warmth.

The Far Away Man said, 'Wait . . . wait!'

8.55 p.m.

The hours of darkness before the day.

The Far Away Man, sleeping or waking, said desperately, 'Wait, please wait . . . !'

Shen.

Sharwood.

Mao.

Oliviera.

The eight yellow pages from International Health Certificates bearing, in the same hand, the names of five Chinese and a Korean, a Burmese and a Japanese.

In his apartment, staring out at the lights of the harbour over Beach Road, Feiffer said softly, 'God . . . !'

And 'knifeteeth'.

And a silver snuff box bearing the crossed bones and death's head of a regiment that had charged at Sebastopol, and . . .

And a box full of outboard motors. Feiffer, rubbing at his face, said softly in the heat, 'God . . . !'

And a face: a face he knew.

His wife and son were still out.

Feiffer, snapping his holstered revolver onto the belt of his clean suit and tapping for a moment at its butt, said softly to the lights, 'Goddamn you! Who are you? Who the hell are you?'

He was his new friend. He had been his only friend. In Australia, before he had come to Hong Kong, before – before the flying ribbons and before – before Shen and Sharwood and Mao and Oliviera and . . .

Before all that he had been his friend.

The Far Away Man shouted, '*Wait!*'

Long ago and far away.

The Far Away Man, his face silent and expressionless, shouted, 'Wait!'

The Far Away Man, weeping, cried out to the boy on the bridge, 'Wait! Please wait! You're supposed to be my brother now!' Shanghai, China. Somewhere in picture books: the boy had come all that way to the wooden bridge and now he was —

The Far Away Man cried out to the boy, 'Please, you're supposed to be my brother! It's the war! You're supposed to be my brother now because of the war!' The Far Away Man shouted, 'Wait!!'

The boy had been evacuated from Shanghai during the war to his house in Sydney and while the war was on, the boy had to be his brother. He had promised.

The Far Away Man, on his veranda, called back across almost forty years to the times before the flying ribbons and all the dead men, 'Harry! Harry Feiffer!'

The Far Away Man called out on that bridge over the harbour, so long ago, on that day, 'Harry! Harry! You *promised*!'

9.01 p.m.

In his fourth-floor apartment on Beach Road, The Far Away Man, readying himself to go out, said softly, desperately, 'Harry, Harry . . . please . . . *Wait!*'

12

On the phone in the Detectives' Room, Feiffer said, 'This is Detective Chief Inspector Feiffer of Yellowthread Street Station. I gather at one stage you used to work in the Department of Pharmaceutical Medicine at Hong Kong University and I wonder if I could trouble you with a few questions?' Auden and Spencer and O'Yee were downstairs with Special Branch and the second monstrous pile of disassembled guns, and in the Detectives' Room, briefly, he was alone. Feiffer said, 'Ma'am?'

'Certainly.' The woman's voice was warm.

'Good.' Feiffer lit a cigarette. His hand was shaking. Feiffer said, 'I've got as part of a case I'm working on eight torn-out pages from International Health Certificate booklets and I wondered if you could tell me –'

The voice said pleasantly, 'I'm sorry, I didn't quite catch your name. Who did you say you were?'

'Feiffer. Detective Chief Inspector Harry Feiffer of –'

The woman's voice said, 'Oh, yes.' She waited.

His hand was shaking. Feiffer said, 'And you see, the names on the pages are all of people of different nationalities and all of them are filled out in the same hand and the stamp of the issuing office has been torn out and –'

Nicola Feiffer said, 'Harry . . .'

'Yes?'

His wife said, 'Are you all right, Harry?'

'Sure. It's just that I thought . . .' Feiffer said, 'Is His Nibs in bed? The brat?'

'Are you all right, Harry?'

'Oh, sure.' Feiffer said, 'I just thought that since you used to be in the pharmaceutical line that I could –'

'I wasn't in the Health Department line.'

'– that I could –' He couldn't stop his hand shaking. Feiffer said desperately, 'You know, that I could charge the call up to the office and –' His breathing was coming hard. The cigarette in his hand would not stop shaking. Feiffer said, 'Nikkie, he's someone I know!'

'Who?'

'I don't know!' Outside, the night was dark and silent. Feiffer said, 'I don't know. I only saw him for a moment and I –'

'Come home, Harry.'

'I can't come home. He's still out there and so far in one day he's killed five people!' Feiffer said desperately, 'And I bloody know him! I know I do! He's someone I *know*!'

'*Who?*'

'I don't know! He isn't the same anymore! He's changed! Everything about him – it's all different – changed! It's like someone you thought was dead and he's come back and you can't place him in the real, living world!' Feiffer said, 'U Ne, Koo, Harada, Yen, Li, Chiang, Tang and a bloody Korean called Kim – who the hell are all these people?'

'What about a connection between the people he's killed?' Nicola Feiffer said helpfully, 'You know, on the detective movies on television –'

'This isn't bloody television! If you look in the laundry basket in the bathroom you'll find my clothes covered in goddamned human blood! It's real! This bastard is going around killing real, living people and there's not a bloody thing I can do to stop him!' Feiffer said, 'The Commander thinks I'm covering up for someone I know!'

'Who are all these people you listed?'

'They're the names on the bloody yellow pages I keep

finding every time he slaughters someone! They're nobodies, ghosts! They're people who don't exist! Eight of them! Eight of them without a single record of their ever being in Hong Kong and nothing but bloody cholera injections and their names all written out in the same hand!' It was stupid. He shouldn't have rung. Feiffer said, 'Look, forget it. I'm sorry. I shouldn't have –' He saw her face and the face of his son, sleeping. Feiffer said, 'I suppose I just wanted to hear your voice.'

There was silence.

Feiffer said, 'Are you there?'

Nicola Feiffer said, 'Maybe they're illiterate, Harry. Maybe that's why somebody else filled in the forms for them.'

'Yeah, maybe they are.'

The yellow pages were spread out on his desk. Feiffer, gazing down at them, said sadly, 'Yeah, maybe they are.'

'He must have been one hell of a linguist to fill out the forms in Chinese, Japanese, Burmese and Korean.' Nicola Feiffer asked curiously, 'How do you know it was all done by the same person?'

How did he know? Feiffer said slowly, 'Because they were done in the same hand.'

'In all those languages?'

'No, in English.'

'Why?'

Why? Feiffer said, 'Because they were– Because they were –' His hand stopped shaking. He saw the lights from his apartment window. He saw the lights flickering and glowing in the night. Feiffer said, 'Because they were all together! Because they weren't eight separate people at all – because they were all together!' He said in sudden triumph, '*Weren't they?*'

'Were they?'

'Yes! I've found them two at a time, but they weren't just – they weren't just –' Feiffer said with sudden hope, 'My God, they weren't eight separate people, they were all together! At one time, all the pages were all together! All the complete books were all together, all in the same place when –' Feiffer said, 'My God! I know who they are!' He was not talking into the phone, he was talking at it. It was clear. It was obvious. Feiffer said to whoever it was that was listening, 'Don't you see? Shen, the shoe shine man and Sharwood and Oliviera and Mao! They all had one thing in common!' It was obvious, stupidly simple: the one possible explanation – the *only* one. Feiffer said, 'What they had in common – Shen with his shoe shine beat along the waterfront and then to the naval base, and Sharwood at the base itself, and Mao the fortune teller for fishermen and private customers and Oliviera with his crates for Australia full of outboard motors – what they had in common was the *sea*!' Feiffer said, 'My God! I know who they are!' And he knew why, at one time they had all been together in Hong Kong and, in theory, in legal reality, in bureaucratic form-filling, why they had never been in Hong Kong and no one had any record of them. Feiffer said, 'They were never here because they didn't set foot in the place because someone had their fucking bloody goddamned health certificates and he was handing them out to shoe shine men and naval officers and bloody fortune tellers and factory managers and God knows who else and stopping them from –' Feiffer said, 'U, Koo, Harada. Yen, Li – all of them – my God, they were' – what else could they have been? – Feiffer said with triumph, 'They were a bloody ship's *crew*! They were moored out in the harbour while they were here and they didn't land! They were a ship's *crew*!'

There was a silence and then Nicola Feiffer said softly, 'Harry . . .'

'Yes?'

There was another silence.

He saw her face.

Feiffer said softly, 'Yes, me too.' He was alone in the Detectives' Room. Feiffer said again, 'Yes, me too.'

He saw her face.

There was no sound as he hung up and, his hand still steady, he put the cigarette down carefully on his ashtray and, for a long while, sat staring down at the spread out arranged little display of yellow pages on his desk.

On the phone in the Detectives' Room, Feiffer said quietly, 'Colonel Graham? Look, I'm sorry to ring you in your quarters after hours but I thought I'd just ask if you've managed to come up with anything else about the late Commander Sharwood that you think might be of any assistance.' He looked at the clock on the wall of the Detectives' Room. It read 11.02. 'I didn't want to ring WO Wong because I had the rather worrying feeling that he might want to rerun the routine of telling me, piano wire pressure by piano wire pressure, just how if he'd had the chance he might have killed Sharwood himself.' Feiffer glanced at his watch. It was in synch with the wall clock. 'I've been onto the Military Police and they confirm everything he told me about you – namely, that you were set up.'

There was the slightest of pauses.

11.03.

Feiffer said pleasantly, 'Colonel, are you there?' Graham had been drinking. Feiffer could hear him breathing heavily into the mouthpiece of the phone as he thought. 'I assume you've heard on the news that a couple more people have been killed? The names on the yellow cards they carried – the Chinese and the Korean and the Burmese names, all of them – they represent a ship's crew.'

He heard Graham draw in his breath to control its sound.

Feiffer said, 'It's the drinks' hour, I know, but policemen are famous for not observing the customs.' The wall clock moved a single click. Feiffer said lightly, 'And apart from that, I imagine it's the sort of resentment that goes "if I haven't got time to have a drink I don't see why he should either".' He said softly into the mouthpiece of the phone, 'I think they were probably smuggling. What do you think?'

He waited.

11.04.

Feiffer said easily, 'Well?'

Graham, at the other end of the line, said suddenly, 'What the hell do you want?' Graham said, 'I've told you what you wanted to know! WO Wong told you what you wanted to know! What the hell are you ringing me for?'

'Company. I'm feeling lonely. I've got all these yellow cards with all these names on them from a ship's crew and I thought "Who do I know who knows anything about ships?" and I thought of you.' Feiffer said, 'Poor old Sharwood. What a pathetic little creature he was. Obviously, if he only took a few dollars worth of bits and pieces of – you know – old wire or broken fuses or a few gold sovereigns with the Queen's head on them from the jolly old Mess funds then, obviously, he was a kleptomaniac – but I wonder why he went to all the trouble of trying to push the blame for his little harmless bouts of kleptomania onto you?' He could hear Graham's breathing again. It was tight. Feiffer said easily, 'Any ideas, Colonel, old man? Blue, old chap? Old cobber, old Digger, old mate, old Sport?'

11.05.

The yellow pages and the snuff box were laid out on his desk. Feiffer said, 'I'm surprised you haven't asked me what they were smuggling. I always thought Australians were direct, blunt, bluff and curious.' Feiffer said, 'I lived there myself for about five or six years and I must say it was one of the features I most admired.' Feiffer said, 'Yes? Do you want me to tell you what they were smuggling, Colonel? Do you want me to give you a list?'

There was no sound from the other end of the line.

Feiffer said tightly, 'Nothing. Six dollars and eighty-five cents: that's what the shoe shine man was smuggling if he was smuggling anything. Or a pair of broken sandals. And the fortune teller – he was smuggling –' He was trying to provoke the man, but there was nothing. 'He was smuggling – he was smuggling a brocade-covered book with a fortune to order marked in it. "Go not as told by others,/ But by other ways go. Knifeteeth." That's what he was smuggling.' The clock moved a half click. 'And Oliviera, why he was smuggling outboard motors to a country that didn't want outboard motors and he was such a good, successful smuggler that each and every one of the final consignment of his motors was still in the factory looking for another buyer!' Feiffer said, 'So who does that leave who was smuggling anything worthwhile?' He paused. 'Well, that just leaves good old Lieutenant Commander The Honourable Julian Sharwood RN.' There was no sound from the other end of the line. Feiffer said, 'That leaves *you*!'

'*I don't know a fucking thing about anything!*'

'Don't you?' Feiffer said, 'Don't you? No? The military bloody mind that could take the horrors of bloody Viet Nam has packed up over a few bits of stolen wire and the non-coms' picnic fund money. Has it really?' Feiffer said, 'No, it hasn't. Wrong country, wrong time. That's not the Australian Army in the 1980s – no, you've got that one wrong. That's the bloody British Sahibs in their billiards room in the bloody 1860s!' Feiffer said, 'The only possible reason all these people could be involved with what's pretty obviously some sort of multi-national scow plying the bloody freight routes of Asia and Australia is that they were smuggling something on it and I can only come up with two or three possibilities as to what it was they smuggled, and for every one of them you need money!' Feiffer said, 'And I don't see how you can buy much of anything worth smuggling if you're walking around with six dollars and eighty-five cents in your pocket or you tell your fortunes in somewhere like Cuttlefish Lane or you sit up late every night in a deserted factory trying to stave off bankruptcy! But I do see how if you've got the run of an entire bloody Stores base the situation's a bit different, and what I want to know from you is this: just what the hell did Sharwood steal?' He gave Graham no chance to reply, 'That the bloody MPs didn't find?'

'It could have been anything!'

'Like what?'

'It could have been –' He was sobering fast. Graham said, 'Tell me how the hell they were smuggling anything! Tell me how!'

'They were smuggling it in Oliviera's outboard motor crates!'

148

'I thought you said all the outboard motors were still here in the Colony!'

'Only the last part of the consignment. Only the final shipment. The Australians cracked down on him and closed off his market months ago and yet – and yet – and yet he kept his own two yellow pages in a sample packing crate marked "Australia". Why? Why if that market had finished and he was looking for new ones why the hell did he still keep it with him in the packing department? For nostalgia? He was keeping it there as a bloody talisman, the same way the shoe shine man kept it on his person and the same way the fortune teller kept his in his precious bloody brocaded book!' Feiffer said, 'Did you hear that on the news? The fortune teller wasn't like Sharwood. He got it twice: once through the head and then a second time through the heart.' Feiffer said, 'See lots of dead bodies in Viet Nam, did you? Ever seen one with half its head infested with flies in a hundred degrees heat? Ever *smell* it?'

'What do you want from me? WO Wong –'

'WO Wong would walk across bloody fire for you! I should have realized it at the time! WO Wong, unlike you and me, is a Chinese, and the Chinese don't have respect for fools and they certainly don't have fantasies about killing them! What the Chinese do is believe in luck and fortune and what WO Wong thinks is that yours took a bad turn through no fault of your own and he's –'

'It wasn't my fault!' Graham said, 'I should have been pensioned off but I've got nowhere else to go. Sharwood took advantage of me – you know the Services – if a bloody officer wants to rip them off all he has to do –'

11.09

Feiffer said quietly, 'Colonel Graham, the size of the crates Oliviera sent to Australia were six foot long by four foot deep by four foot wide. Don't make me ring my Commander to authorize a hundred men to come down there and tear your warehouses apart brick by brick to find what you've got that size.'

'You don't have that sort of authority!'

'Don't I?' Feiffer said, 'Six by four by four. It goes in a wooden crate six by four by four.'

'You're just testing me! It's just because it's a ship and this is Hong Kong – that's why you think it's smuggling. You haven't got any proof! It's just a theory! And you haven't got the faintest iota of solid evidence to back it up! You've just gone through the list of people this fucking maniac has killed and you've tried to put it all together with these fucking yellow cards and what you've come up with is the fact that if anyone had access to anything valuable it had to be Sharwood!' Graham said with rising confidence, 'What about this bloody shoe shine man – why the hell couldn't he have stolen something?'

'Because he was just the bloody messenger between all the conspirators and because if he'd stolen anything he wouldn't have bothered about getting involved with ships and bloody naval officers and factory managers – he would have gone straight to the nearest bloody pawn shop and sold what he had and retired to the New Territories with his plans for a bloody duck farm! And Oliviera wouldn't have been sitting in his office night after night sweating his guts out the way he was – he would have been sampling the delights of his girlfriend's loins nonstop on the beaches of fucking Bali! And the fortune teller wouldn't have been in Cuttlefish Lane!' Feiffer said, 'No, it's Sharwood. Sharwood was the one who provided the goods and Oliviera was the one who sent them!'

'Why the hell don't I just tell you to shove it straight up your arse and hang up?'

Feiffer said, 'Yeah, why don't you?' Feiffer said again, 'Six by four by four foot deep –'

11.10 p.m.

He was close. He knew it. He was so close.

Feiffer shouted, '*Graham, what the hell did Sharwood take?*'

'Ask the ship's crew!'

'I can't find the ship's crew!'

Graham said quietly, 'Oh, God . . .'

150

'Why?' He paused. In the Detectives' Room the time was ticking away. The Far Away Man was in the streets, killing and killing. Feiffer said suddenly, 'Why? Why can't I find the ship's crew?'

There was a silence.

'Graham?'

Nothing.

Feiffer shrieked, '*Graham!*'

Graham said – There was a pause. On the other end of the line, Feiffer heard his breath catch. Graham said –

Feiffer said, 'Six by four by –'

'WO Wong . . .'

'Forget WO Wong! Six by four by bloody four foot deep!' The clock clicked. Feiffer said –

'A silver snuff box!' He was finished. It was over. All the drink in the world was useless. It was done. Graham, breaking, shouted down the line, 'A silver snuff box for a man who didn't take snuff!'

'What the hell are you talking about?'

'I'm talking about – about –' He was sniffling, in tears. Behind him, Feiffer heard the sound of a bottle or glass falling to the floor. Graham said, 'A silver snuff box for a man who didn't take snuff! It was no fantasy – we were going to kill him: Wong and I – we were going to –' Graham said, 'It's all too late! If you can't find the ship's crew it's all too late!' He ordered Feiffer, 'Look at the silver snuff box! Look hard at it! Look at it! He used to leave it on my bloody desk!' Graham shrieked, 'Don't you see? They didn't smuggle anything! You stupid bastard, that's what we thought too, but if the crew's –' Graham said, 'Six by four by four foot deep – you want to know what he took and set me up for? It wasn't the money or the bits and pieces! That's what the MPs thought, but Wong and I, we –' Graham said, 'It was Wong's responsibility too, not just mine – we would both have gone! It would have been the end of both of us!' Graham said, 'A bloody Mark 9/52 with a thousand pounds of H.E. RDX complex in it, that's what he took!'

'What?'

'All up weight two thousand four hundred and ninety six pounds – but he didn't take all that, just the bit that mattered!' Graham said, 'That's what they sent off to bloody Australia on their bloody ship – if that's where they sent it – that's what it was: a Mark 9/52 with –' Graham said, 'The silver snuff box where he kept his yellow crew cards – don't you see? That's why you can't find the crew – because they're not coming back!' Graham said, 'A Mark 9 Torpedo warhead! With eleven hundred pounds of RDX high explosive packed into it!' Graham said, 'Smuggling – arseholes! That isn't the insignia of the good old bloody nineteenth-century revolver in the billiards room 17th/21st Lancers engraved on his snuff box! Look at it again! The engraving's new!' Graham said, 'What that is is a skull and bloody crossbones!' Graham shrieked, 'They didn't smuggle anything you bloody fool! Not on that ship! They didn't smuggle anything on that bloody ship!' Graham said, 'No! Can't you see it? They were *pirates*! What they did to that ship was *kill* it!'

11.45 p.m.

In the Detectives' Room, Feiffer said softly, 'Oh my God . . .'

Go not as told by others,
But by other ways go.
Knifeteeth.

Graham said softly, 'Harry, I don't know why . . . I swear to God, I don't know why . . .'

Some dark presence watching by my bed,
The awful image of a nameless dread.

He had seen him. For the briefest of moments in the half light, he had seen him. Long ago, far away.

'Harry, Harry, you *promised* . . .'

It was him. It could be no one else.

The last person in the world . . .

Feiffer said softly, 'Oh my God . . .'

He had seen him. For the briefest of moments in the half

152

light as he killed and killed and killed, he had seen him and he had known who he was.

The Far Away Man.

The last person in the world . . . the *only* one.

It was Charlie Corey.

11.45 p.m.

For a moment, across the traffic from Yellowthread Street Station, The Far Away Man paused.

His eyes were pale and distant. They were not real.

He saw only the blur of lights and movement. He heard only garbled sounds.

There was a single spot of blood at the corner of his mouth.

He was no longer connected to the outside world. He was moving only between cardinal points in his head.

It did not occur to him to wonder why he had stopped.

Touching at the spot of blood with his finger, feeling the weight of the gun under his coat in his belt, The Far Away Man, relentlessly, unstoppably, moved on.

13

On Beach Road, Auden already had the SG loaded riot gun out of the boot of his car and he was looking up at the apartments as he fed shells quickly and expertly into the magazine. At the front of the car, O'Yee, also looking up, said incredulously, 'You've been doing what, Harry?' He couldn't believe his ears. 'You've been carrying his picture around in your wallet? A picture of Corey?' He took the snapshot from Feiffer and tried to look at it in the reflected lights of the harbour. It showed Feiffer and his wife and another man and a woman and two children standing together somewhere, but he could not make out the man in the poor light as anything other than a blur. 'Who is he? Why the hell is he killing all these people?'

Spencer came around from the side door of the car drawing his weapon and Feiffer ordered him, 'You! With Auden!' He saw O'Yee still waiting for an answer. 'He's Charlie Corey. His firm did the insurance on the ship they sank!' He ordered Spencer, 'You and Phil take the elevator to the fourth floor and secure the corridor!' He began moving himself towards the entrance to the apartments taking O'Yee with him. Feiffer said, 'He worked out who they were and how they did it – that's why he's killing them! He worked out how they sank the ship and he worked out who it was and now he's doing something about it! He worked for the Hong Bay branch of Lloyds and he was the one who actually did the insurance on the ship! The shoe shine man – the messenger – Sharwood, Oliviera, the fortune teller . . . he's worked it all out and he knows who each of them was and now he's killing them!' Feiffer, taking the apartment stairs two at a time, said, 'Charlie Corey.' He nodded to the photograph still in O'Yee's hand. (O'Yee, keeping up with him, had no time to look at it.) 'Go not as told by others, But by other ways go: it was a change in course. The number twenty-one was the lucky number Mao foisted on, probably, the Captain of the ship based on some garbage he invented when he came to have his fortune told and what it meant was that the ship should make an unscheduled detour to its course to avoid – Knifeteeth!' Feiffer said, 'To avoid *sharks*!' When you realized what it was there was no other possibility. Feiffer said, 'It's the one thing Chinese sailors are afraid of above all else: death by water and the dismemberment of their bodies.'

They reached the second-floor landing. The corridor facing it was brightly lit but deserted. Feiffer said, 'He probably told that poor dumb bastard to take his ship hundreds of miles off the normal shipping lanes, and then when the torpedo Oliviera had secreted in his hold along with a consignment of motors went sky high any rescue party that came along later to find survivors wouldn't even be looking in the right area!' He halted for a moment. There was only one elevator in that section of the apartments and with the changing of the lights above the door, it was moving down to Auden and Spencer on the ground. Feiffer said, 'I thought he'd left the Colony months ago. After he – I kept trying to ring him or drop by to see him but there was never anyone at home and I thought –' The elevator lights reached the ground floor and stopped as Auden and Spencer must have piled in. Feiffer, moving again, said, 'Come on! Come on!'

O'Yee, trying to catch up, said, 'But why, Harry, why? If he was just the insurance man why is he –' Feiffer was ahead of him on the stairs. O'Yee, running after him, feeling like a little boy trying to catch up with an older brother, demanded, 'If he knows what happened why the hell didn't he just tell *you*?' He got no reply. Feiffer reached the next landing, glanced down to the corridor to check it was clear, and carried on up the stairs to the next. 'The witnesses said he was –' O'Yee called up with his legs aching with the climb '– said he looked *crazy*!' He called out, 'Harry, what the hell do you know about this that I don't? Why is he killing these people?' He reached the next landing and then the next and almost ran into the muzzle of Auden's riot gun as Auden came out of the elevator and covered the corridor. O'Yee, seeing Feiffer at a door in the corridor, called out, 'Harry, *what the hell's going on?*' He saw Feiffer at the door as the cocking bolt of Auden's riot gun came back with a clatter and lights began going on under the door jambs. There were people stirring in the apartments on either side of the door. Lights began coming on under the door jambs. O'Yee heard sounds, voices. O'Yee, with the photo- graph still in his hand, said warningly, 'Harry –'

Feiffer said, 'Shoot the lock off!' He stood back.

O'Yee said, 'Harry!' He saw Feiffer's eyes. O'Yee said, 'Harry, this isn't the way to –'

Auden, hesitating, said, 'Boss?'

'It's steel lined!' Feiffer, his eyes blazing, looked at Auden. Auden was still hesitating. Feiffer said, 'Goddamnit, I was the one who advised him to have the door put in!' Feiffer said, 'Put the muzzle against the side of the jamb at the lock socket and pull the bloody trigger!' Behind the door was The Far Away Man. Feiffer said, 'Now!'

The photograph was still in O'Yee's hand. It was all happen- ing too quickly. O'Yee, moving fast to stop Auden, said, 'Harry, if you haven't been able to raise him for months he could have *moved*!' He saw the muzzle of the riot gun come up. In the other apartments, people were stirring. Any moment they would stream out into the corridor to see what the noise was. O'Yee said, 'Wait!' He still had the photograph in his hand. In the bright lights of the corridor, he looked down at it. O'Yee, rooted to the spot, said, 'No! Wait! It isn't –!'

People were stirring. Along the corridor doors began open- ing. Spencer said warningly, 'Harry –'

Feiffer ordered, 'Do it!'

Auden, obedient to the end, said, 'Right!' and in a shattering explosion that blew out two of the overhead lights in the corridor and sent shock-waves up and down its length in an almost visible wave, pulled the trigger and took the door straight off in a single, merging crash.

O'Yee said, 'Wait!' They were all going in, guns drawn. In the corridor, chasing them, O'Yee, with the picture still in his hand, said desperately, 'No! *No!*' Thin, fair-haired, dying, crazy, unreal: The Far Away Man.

O'Yee, going into the darkened room a second after them, called out in horror, 'Harry, it isn't him! It isn't him!' The apartment was dark. He heard people scrabbling around for the light switch. In all the other apartments along the corridor people had started screaming and opening doors.

Into the pitch black darkness of the apartment, into the whole wrongness of the place, O'Yee said desperately, 'Harry, the man in this picture –!' He called out to no response, 'Harry, he weighs over two hundred and eighty pounds!' The lights came on and he saw Feiffer's face.

O'Yee said in total, impotent horror, 'Harry, it isn't him! He's too fat! He's too bloody *fat!*'

It had all gone wrong.

O'Yee said hopelessly, 'Harry! Harry, the man in the photograph – *it isn't him!*'

It was him. He saw him.

On the waterfront, near the great spice warehouse and jetties on Aberdeen Road, The Far Away Man shaded his eyes and nodded.

It was him.

He was moving.

There were great banks of floodlights on each of the concrete jetties between the warehouses illuminating him as he walked, and The Far Away Man, watching, knew it was him.

He was the last. He saw him.

Pak.

He saw Pak walking along the concrete concourses between the warehouses, pass over a little Bailey bridge and, pausing for a moment, glance down to one of the man-made canals between the warehouses where the barges were.

Pak.

It was him.

The Far Away Man looked at his watch.

1.47 a.m.

It was him.

The Far Away Man watched as he walked through great circles of light the floodlights made on the deserted concrete jetties. He could almost hear his footsteps.

Like a shadow, a spirit, Pak was walking at an even, unrelenting pace through the pools of light towards him. The Far Away Man saw him pass across one of the Bailey bridges and pause to look down from it to the moored silk barges below.

1.47 a.m.

It was him.

The Far Away Man, drawing his gun, went soundlessly towards the lights to wait.

In the apartment, Auden, leaning down with the riot gun still in his hands, said in triumph, 'You got him, Harry, you got him!' On the coffee table in front of him there was the open gun box. Auden, reading the label on the lid, said, 'Charlemont, Jeunet Et Neveu, Rue De La Caserne, 16, Bruxelles – it's a bloody de luxe model gun box for a silver-plated presentation, single-shot pistol!' There were cartridges in their compartments at the bottom left-hand corner of the box, all gleaming brass. Auden, picking up one of them and reading the headstamp, said, 'Thirty-eight S&W – that's the one!' He looked across to where Feiffer was watching him from the centre of the room, 'You got him, Boss!' He saw Spencer also in the centre of the room on his hands and knees at a pile of cardboard cartons, 'What have you got?'

Spencer said, 'Clothes. Suits. Grey suits and shirts and

underwear, all brand new' – he held up a folded receipt – 'All delivered within the last two or three weeks. It's him, Harry.' He opened another carton and pulled out a rumpled grey suit with blood spots on its sleeves and shoulders. Spencer said, 'It's him. You've got him. It's him.'

He still had the photograph in his hand. The apartment looked bare, except for the cartons and the gun box, untouched for years. There was dust on the ceiling and in the carpet. O'Yee, glancing at Feiffer, asked Spencer, 'What size? What size are the suits?' He saw Spencer look through the labels on the shirts and the coats.

Spencer said, 'No size. They're tailored, done on order.' He lifted one of the coats up and put it against his own chest. 'They're small to medium: for a tall, thin man –' Spencer, looking up, said, 'Who is he, Harry?'

He got no response. Feiffer, jerking his thumb, said quickly, 'The kitchen's through there, and off that are the two bedrooms. The one on the right is the master bedroom and the one on the left –'

O'Yee said, 'It isn't him!'

'It is him!'

'It can't be!' O'Yee saw Auden start to go towards the kitchen and bedroom area with the riot gun and he ordered him, 'Wait!' O'Yee said, 'There isn't anyone here! There hasn't been anyone here for months – for what? – four months? *Has there, Harry?*'

Feiffer said, 'Corey's been here!' He nodded to Auden, 'Check the kitchen.'

'How the hell can it be Corey? Corey's the size of bloody Fatty Arbuckle!' O'Yee, still grasping the photograph, demanded, 'How the hell can it be him? It isn't him!' He saw Feiffer's face.

'It's Corey!'

'It isn't Corey!' O'Yee twisting the picture in his hand and thrusting it under Feiffer's face, said, 'Look! Look! That's Corey! And –'

Feiffer said, 'And this is bloody Hong Kong!'

'What the hell does that mean?'

Feiffer said to Auden and Spencer, 'Check the kitchen. All you'll find in there is dust, but check it anyway and then –' Feiffer, shaking his head, said, 'I've told you! You asked and I've told you! All right? Understand? You're supposed to be the old bloody China Hand! You asked and I told you – it's Corey! It's Corey and –'

O'Yee snarling, yelled, 'What? And this is Hong Kong? *What the hell does that mean?*'

From the kitchen, Auden yelled out, 'Nothing.' There was a series of crashing noises as he and Spencer opened and shut cupboard doors and deep-freezer lids, then a series of thumping sounds as more cupboards were opened. Auden called out, 'Harry, are you sure anybody lives here?'

From the kitchen Spencer called out, 'Harry, what did this man *eat?*'

O'Yee said, 'Harry –' He stopped. New, tailored clothes in boxes on the floor. O'Yee said, 'Harry –' And blood. All the witnesses had reported blood on his mouth and all his hair had come out when the Factotum had grabbed him and all the witnesses said he had been – O'Yee said again, 'Harry –' He had read all the reports. Mui: the jade shop owner, he had said he had thought, from his face that the man was – O'Yee, with a strange feeling in the pit of his stomach, said, hoping it was not true, 'Harry . . . ?' He looked at Feiffer's face.

'Yeah.' His face was not blank. It was drained of colour. Feiffer, nodding, said sadly, 'Yeah, his wife and children were on the ship.' He was still standing at the entrance to the corridor where the kitchen and the bedrooms were, afraid to go any further. Feiffer said, 'His wife and his two daughters.' He looked away. 'I – I kept trying to contact him, but –' He glanced down at the floor, 'But I could never get an answer.' Feiffer said, 'Hong Kong. One lousy person in a bloody non-stop crowd of people . . .' Feiffer said quietly, 'Charlie Corey. Old jolly, jumbo, elephantine Charlie Corey.' Feiffer said, 'The ship was called the *Peking Star*. They – they were originally booked on another ship, but at the last moment there was a – there was a problem with their luggage and they –' Feiffer said sadly, 'They were going back home to Australia. Charlie had a few months left with the insurance company and he thought they could go back early by sea and set things up for when he came and, ah –' Feiffer, still looking down said, 'He was in Japan at the time and when he came back –' Feiffer said, 'Bloody Hong Kong.' Feiffer said, 'When he came back they were all dead!'

From the passage Auden called, 'Nothing in the main bedroom. The other door's locked. Do you want it down?'

Feiffer, looking up, said, 'Yeah. Break it down.' He looked at O'Yee and for an awful moment it looked as if there were tears in his eyes.

Feiffer said quietly, touching O'Yee on the shoulder, 'It was about four months ago, and since then –'

O'Yee said quietly, 'And since then he's been starving himself to death, *hasn't he*?'

There was no response. For a long while, until the crash of the bedroom door being broken in came along the corridor in a single *crack*, Feiffer went on staring into O'Yee's face.

Auden called out, 'Harry! Come and look at this!'

It was the children's bedroom.

Somewhere, out at sea, they were all long dead.

Feiffer, bracing himself, said quietly as he began to go down the passageway, 'Christopher, come with me, would you?' He began to go down the corridor towards the room with leaden feet.

At the open door, Feiffer, his eyes closed, afraid of what he might see, said in sudden desperation, 'Christopher, for the love of God, don't let me go in there alone!'

He was there. He was in place.

1.55 a.m.

He only had a little while to wait. The time was immaterial.

The Far Away Man, in the awful loneliness of his life, said fiercely, 'Come and get it, Pak, you murdering bastard, *come and fucking get it*!'

161

He was the last.

The Far Away Man, unconscious of time, awaited him in the light.

Cinderella, Snow White, Pluto, Mickey, Goofy, Bambi. Below the ribbons, on the coloured lampshade in the childrens' room, they were all going around and around in a world of glowing, coloured lights, chasing each other at an unending, child-giggling pace around and around and around. There was a single low-watt bulb burning in the lamp keeping the lamp-shade alive and moving and, below it on the floor around it, dozens and dozens of burned-out bulbs and fresh bulbs in boxes ready for the display should it stop for even the briefest moment. There were ribbons glued to the lampshade, each on the neck or shoulder of a favourite character on the shade, scorched and tattered at the ends with the heat. The lamp was still going. The lamp had been going for a very long time.

In the room, Feiffer said, 'Carol and Nicola. His wife's name and mine: his children.' There was a bunk bed in one corner of the room, both the beds made tightly and freshly as if their owners had only made them this morning. It was where he lived. In the room, Feiffer said, 'He . . . um . . .'

Auden was at the door with the riot gun still in his hand. O'Yee, turning to him, said, 'Wait outside.' He saw Spencer touch him on the shoulder and propel him gently backwards out into the corridor. O'Yee, glancing at Feiffer's face, said softly, 'Harry . . .'

'Yeah.' The ribbons fascinated him. There was a single smell in the room, just one. It was the smell of talc, lavender: the freshly bathed and shampooed smell of children in fresh pyjamas. Feiffer, moving forward, went towards the bed where The Far Away Man had been living and touched it and found no smell of him there at all. Feiffer, touching at his face, said softly, 'Yeah . . .' The lower bed was tightly made, but you could see where a fully grown person had been in it from the wrinkles. Wedged into the wall, there was a tiny plastic Donald Duck, a forgotten treasure, a souvenir from somewhere imbued, with the death of its owner, with magical, important, totemic properties. Feiffer said softly, 'He was a man who always wanted more from people than they could give.' He touched at the model with his fingertips and then let it fall gently back into its secret niche against the bed, 'He came to Hong Kong because of me.' He touched at the model again and then, again, let it go. 'Then, when he met Carol and —' Feiffer said suddenly, 'They killed everything he had and now he's killing them!' There was not another single object in the room: no clothes, no pictures, nothing. Everything had gone with the children on the ship for their new life in Australia. Feiffer said, 'He insured the ship. It was his job — and then, when it went down, somehow he must have found out and now —' His breathing was tight, hard. The room was suffocating him. 'And now, one by one, without any mercy, one by one he's catching up with them with his bloody gun and sending them all to Hell!' Feiffer said fiercely, 'Wouldn't you do the same? *Wouldn't you?*'

'The yellow pages, Harry —'

'The yellow pages are the credentials of the bloody murder gang he's killing off! The yellow cards were given out to the members of the gang so that when the insurance for the ship was claimed by the owner every member of the club who'd done anything — from the highest to the bloody lowest — from Shen to bloody Sharwood — every member would have something tangible to prove that the owner knew the ship wasn't going to arrive at its destination!' Feiffer said angrily, 'Who the hell else do you think would have access to the health certificates of the crew except the Captain and the owner?' Feiffer, clenching and unclenching his fist, said, shaking, 'And the Captain's dead, isn't he? So it was the owner! He gave the members of the club each two yellow cards because there wasn't any possibility that the ship's crew would need them when they disembarked in Australia because those poor, doomed bastards weren't going to get to Australia! The only place they were going was straight down!'

'Harry, if you knew Corey that well and you knew —'

Feiffer said, 'Pak! C. F. bloody Pak!' Feiffer said, 'My God, I've actually met him! The owner of the ship. That's how Corey worked it out. He must have been suspicious. He must have gone back through his files or talked to people who knew him or –' Feiffer said, 'He worked it out a piece at a time exactly the same way I did: a piece at a time, bit by bit! In this room, lying here at night, watching the lamp – a little at a time – piece by piece, putting it together, dying a day at a time!' Feiffer said with unbridled transmitted hatred, 'Pak! And he's waiting for him somewhere right now with the silver gun – a souvenir from God knows where, something bought or begged from someone on another ship – something he wanted so badly he must have got down on his knees and begged for! Something he –' He ordered O'Yee, 'Christopher, get on the phone. Find Pak's address and if he isn't there talk to one of his servants and find out where he is!' He saw O'Yee hesitate. Auden was at the door with his riot gun, looking ready.

Feiffer, trying to keep his eyes from the glowing lamp, said quickly, 'Do it now! Hurry!'

It was 2.09 a.m.

Feiffer said, 'Hurry! For God's sake, hurry!'

'*Harry, you promised . . .*'

Feiffer, desperate, said, 'Please! Hurry!'

14

That day on the bridge had been the last day. As the barge had gone beneath the metal spans of the bridge in the harbour on a brilliant, sun-lit Sydney morning, that day had been the last. It had been the last day of his childhood, of his happiness. The war was over. There had been first one atomic bomb on Japan and then another – on cities with strange unpronounceable names – and at the end of it, other places with other names were free and all the people who had fled from them were going back.

He was leaving. Crossing the bridge to go somewhere to take a ship to one of those strange places – to Shanghai – his friend was leaving.

Harry was leaving.

His friend. He was going, leaving.

Beneath the brilliant banks of lights on the jetties by the great spice warehouses of Hong Kong, The Far Away Man said to himself, 'Harry, wait . . .'

He was going. The war was over and he was going back, away, and he would never see him again.

In his thirteen-year-old mind, The Far Away Man said softly, 'Harry, you promised you'd always be my friend.'

The Far Away Man said softly, 'A Mustang, Harry.' Beneath him, on the bridge, half covered up in a tarpaulin, there was an American Mustang fighter going off to war.

There was no war. The war was finished and the Mustang, travelling at the speed of a slow, flat, bubbling-engined barge, was merely going off to be scrapped.

The Far Away Man touched at his eyes. In front of him, in Hong Kong, lit up in the glow of the lights, there was another bridge spanning a little canal between the warehouses for the barges that took the spices out to the ships moored in the harbour, the spices all in wooden tea chests and barrels with all the strange names of China on them: the names of the war.

He saw a barge moored below the bridge.

He was hurting. Standing in the glow of the lights as a single, stark silhouette on the grey, deserted jetty, he was hurting. His eyes were going. He saw the bridge merge and become another bridge and one of the long, flat barges moored beneath it became another barge with a covered-over Mustang on board it – then it ebbed and changed and it was itself.

The Far Away Man had his gun in his hand and he looked down at it and unknotted his fingers from its butt with his free hand. All the joints in his hand hurt. He touched at the knuckles and they were tender and painful.

The Far Away Man said softly, 'I could have done it. I could have gone back to Australia with Carol and the children and this time I could have been happy.'

He forced himself to move towards the bridge, a step at a time.

He hurt. He grimaced in pain.

The Far Away Man said, 'I'm not a child anymore – I –' His father had been killed in the war of the Mustangs and the barges and the places with strange names. The Far Away Man said, 'I was lonely, I –' The Far Away Man said, *'This time I could have been happy!'* He saw, way across the bridge and into the distance the lights of junks and sampans moored in the typhoon shelter on Aberdeen Road. The Far Away Man shrieked, 'PAK!!'

There was no sound.

The Far Away Man, with the ribbons and light of the lamp in his children's room turning and turning in his mind, said

166

without words, 'We were going back. We were going back home, all of us. We had a life together. We had –' The Far Away Man, seeing the lights on the boats and junks tighten into a brilliant intensity said, '*PAK!!*'

He was moving towards the bridge: a single, stark outline in the wash of the brilliant overhead lights.

The Far Away Man shrieked, '*Pak!*'

Ribbons. And sounds. And smells. The smell of talc and shampoo: lavender – the smell of small, washed children waiting for – He had been careful, every night he had spent there, not to disturb the beds. Night by night, alternately, he had slept first in the top bed and then, the next night, in the lower.

There had been a single, cheap, plastic toy wedged in his younger daughter's bed – in Nikkie's bed: it was just some useless thing she had thought so little of she had left it to be thrown out.

All he had.

His children.

Everything.

It was something a six-year-old had thought so little of she had not even bothered to –

He reached the bridge and mounted its steel steps. Far away, along the jetties he could see the lights of the sampans and junks moored in the typhoon shelter.

Of all those lights he saw a single light. It was where Pak was.

In the cooling of the night air, the knuckles on The Far Away Man's hand hurt and he rubbed at them. He thought he called out in pain.

His head was an empty space marked out by only cardinal points, points to be arrived at.

Shen.

Sharwood.

Mao.

Oliviera.

He had arrived at all those points.

He was alone.

In the last night, at the last of those cardinal points, he was alone.

The Far Away Man, watching the lights on the boats, standing on the bridge, looked down into the harbour water of the canal. It was filled with the cries of the drowning. The little, useless toy on the bed, at nights, had been all he had.

He stopped.

His eyes were clear and, in the distance, he saw a light.

It was Pak. It was a door opening in the wheelhouse of a boat. He was coming.

The Far Away Man, touching at his gun, said softly, 'Yes . . .'

There was no sound.

2.11 a.m.

On the bridge, The Far Away Man, with all the pain gone, at his last cardinal point, drew his breath and waited.

2.11 a.m.

Way off, leaving the boat to step down to the first of the concrete jetties, as if he had all the time in the world, he saw Pak coming towards him to die.

2.11 a.m.

At the culmination of his life, like the outline of a statue, The Far Away Man waited.

On the deck of junk number N8793 moored in the Aberdeen Road typhoon shelter at mooring A615, Bullet Money Bao, seeing his roulette wheel coming out of the wheelhouse in Auden's hands, shouted in panic, 'I don't know!'

Feiffer ordered Auden, 'Drop it!'

Auden dropped it. The wheel smashed into a thousand pieces.

Bullet Money Bao said, 'Aaiiya!' He looked at O'Yee. O'Yee had Auden's riot gun and was pointing it in the direction of the armful of ivory gambling markers Spencer was bringing out of the wheelhouse. Bullet Money Bao said, 'They're not what you think they are! They're antiques! They're not gambling chips, they're —'

'Where's Pak?'

'I don't know! Who's Pak? I've never heard of —'

Feiffer said, 'Bill —!'

Spencer dropped the markers and trod on them.

'If I knew I'd tell you!' He saw Auden start to go back inside the wheelhouse for more equipment. 'I don't know! I don't run a gambling game, I'm just a collector of —' Bullet Money Bao, seeing Auden go back in for a wall safe in the wheelhouse, shrieked, 'Don't touch my silver!'

Feiffer said, 'Where's Pak? We know he was here. Where is he?'

It wasn't much of a wall safe. It was a cavity in the wall. There was a crash and Auden had it open. Auden shouted out, 'Silver! Thai bullet money ingots! Dozens and dozens of them — they're all about an ounce each!' There was a series of crashes as another piece of the not so good wall cavity became more of a cavity. Auden yelled, 'I can see where he got his name! This place is lousy with ingots of —' There was another crash. Auden yelled, 'Gold!'

Bao, hopping about on the deck, shouted, 'You need a warrant!' He looked at Feiffer's face. They didn't need a warrant. Bao shouted, 'I'm a collector! I collect old roulette wheels and gambling equipment and chips and I —'

Auden shouted, 'Platinum!'

'And I collect coins!' Bao, hopping, said, 'I don't know where he is! There wasn't a game tonight! I —' He felt Feiffer's hand grip him by the shirt and start to propel him towards the railings, 'You're not going to throw me over —'

'Where is he?'

'He's gone!'

'Where?'

'I don't know!'

Feiffer said, 'Phil, get all that stuff together —'

'It's my fortune! It's how I save my money! There's nothing illegal about having ingots and —'

Feiffer said, 'And throw it all over the side!'

'No!'

'Where's Pak?' Feiffer said, 'We know he was here. Where is he and what did he want from you?'

'Nothing!'

Feiffer said, 'Phil –'

Auden came out of the wheelhouse like Midas carrying his day's expenses of fifteen pounds of glittering, glowing precious metals.

Bao said, 'He didn't want anything from me! I want something from him!' The armful of glittering wealth went upwards in Auden's hands. Auden said, 'Boy, are some fish down there going to get a headache!' Bao shouted, 'He owes me money! He said he was going to pay!' Bullet Money Bao said, 'No! No!'

'Why was he here?'

'He owes me money!'

'How was he going to pay if he doesn't have any money?' Feiffer still had the man gripped by the shirt as the ingots glittered in Auden's upraised arms, 'You know what the bastard did, don't you! you know he –'

'I don't know anything!' He heard the first plop as one of the one ounce ingots of Thai silver went over the side. 'He came here to reassure me, that's all! He owes me money! He's owed me money for months! He came here to –' There was another plop and then another. Bao said, '*He wanted something from my safe! He wanted his marker!*'

There was another plop.

Bao, hopping, said, '*No!*' He looked at Feiffer and tried to pull himself away. He saw something glitter and then slap against the water. He forgot what he was going to say. Spencer had the broken ivory markers and was shying them across the water like stones. Bao said, 'Look, look! If there was any illegal gambling going on, why would I have –' There were more plops and more slapping sounds as the ingots and ivory markers each worth approximately the same – a fortune – went into the drink. '*I gave him back his marker so he could pay me!*'

Feiffer said, 'What marker?' He saw Auden raise the rest of

the armful of metal and tense himself to hurl it into Davey Jones' Locker. Feiffer ordered him, 'Wait!' He demanded, 'What marker?'

'The insurance policy! The insurance policy for the ship! He lost a ship and he was waiting on the insurance pay out and he gave me the policy as security on his debts!' Bao, seeing the fruit of his life's usury about to disappear forever into the South China Sea, said, 'The insurance policy! I've been keeping it as collateral until –'

Feiffer said, 'Until what?'

'Until it was paid out!' Bao said, 'It's being paid out today – in a few hours – at nine o'clock! He was here to collect the policy so he could –' He saw Auden still tensed with the ingots in his upraised arms, 'You can't prove any of this is the profits from –'

'Where is he now?'

'He's gone!'

'Where?'

'I don't know where!'

Feiffer said to Auden, 'Chuck it in!'

'There!' Bao managed a pointed finger, 'There! By the spice warehouses!' Bao, looking back and forth between the warehouses and the silver, said desperately, 'There! Look! In the name of heaven, there!' Bao said, 'To his car in the old car park behind –' His finger was pointing down at the banks of lights on the jetties in the distance. Bao said, 'There! Look! You can see him! He's almost on that bridge there with your other man!'

Feiffer said, 'What other man?' He turned and peered into the glowing floodlights two hundred yards away. He could see nothing. Feiffer said, 'What other man?'

Bao said, 'There! Look! Your other man! Your other cop! On the bridge! There! Look! There's Pak and you can see your other man on the bridge going forward to meet him!' Bao said, 'I didn't have anything to do with anything!'

From the bow, O'Yee, scanning the area with his eyes, yelled, 'Harry! I see him! It's Corey!'

Feiffer, moving, said, 'Phil!' The bridge was two hundred yards down the jetties. It was too narrow for the car. Feiffer, starting down the gangplank, yelled, 'Phil, leave that stuff and come on!'

Bao said, 'No! No!'

There was a cascade of splashing metal.

Auden said, '*Oops!*'

He was a moment behind O'Yee and Feiffer and Spencer. Making it down the slimy gangplank onto the mooring jetty, he began to run after them towards the lights.

The lights behind him were burning with a humming sound. They were heavy with accumulated intense power. On his back, The Far Away Man felt their heat. On the bridge, The Far Away Man, waiting, touched at the spot of blood on his mouth and felt the heat of the lights on his back.

He was coming.

Pak.

He heard his footsteps as he mounted the steel steps to the little bridge and began to come over.

It was 2.14 a.m. and he had reached the final moment, and The Far Away Man, drawing in his breath, felt that a great release was almost upon him.

'There! There!' Feiffer, running, saw him. He saw Corey. There were three bridges across canals to cross before he got to him. He counted them as he ran: one – he heard the wooden slats on the iron girders banging and creaking as he went – two – it was a firmer, newer bridge – it made no sound –

He saw the lights behind the third bridge: great, pylon-mounted floodlamps, their bulbs giving off variegated blue and yellow sunspots of light as they glowed with power in the blackness of the night.

There was a dash of only seventy or eighty yards to the final bridge. Feiffer, trying to catch his breath, yelled –

He could get no power from his lungs. He ran in terrible, tight silence.

He saw him. He saw Corey. He saw him.

The lights were on his back. He was in the lights, rising out of them like a Nemesis. He was there, a silhouette: different, unidentifiable. *He was the same.*

The Far Away Man, the same man but different, his hand shaking as he raised the long silver gun in the brilliant white light, said softly, 'Hullo, Pak. Remember me? I've changed a little, but it's still me.'

He saw Pak's face. He had forgotten what a little weasel's face it was. Behind the thick lensed spectacles, he saw Pak's eyes widen.

The Far Away Man, taking a single step forward, his voice at last there, said quietly, 'Hullo, Pak.' His voice was soft and conversational. The Far Away Man said conversationally, 'I believe the insurance company is going to make you a rich man in just a few hours.'

The Far Away Man said, 'What a pity for you that you won't live that long.'

The Far Away Man, moving closer to the centre of the bridge, said with his hands shaking on the gun, 'Pak, in exactly three seconds, I'm going to shoot you down like a dog.'

The heat from the lights was beating down on his back.

The eyes were pale and unreal and there was a single spot of blood on The Far Away Man's mouth.

His hair was coming out in clumps.

The Far Away Man did not sweat.

He was Death.

On the bridge, with the lights glowing and discharging behind him like the illuminations to the entrance to Hell, The Far Away Man, the gun shaking with power in his outstretched hand, began squeezing the trigger.

COREY

At the third bridge Feiffer yelled, '*Corey!*' He heard O'Yee and Auden and Spencer behind him, but the bridge was no good for them: there was only room for one. He saw Pak down on his knees in front of The Far Away Man, his hands covering his face, babbling. He saw the long silver gun glitter in the light. He saw Corey's face. The eyes were gone, they were dark sockets. They were looking down at the back of Pak's head where the gun was. The hand holding the gun was shaking with the effort.

Feiffer yelled out, 'Charlie – *no!*' He heard a clatter behind him and saw Auden wrench the riot gun out of Spencer's hands at the run and pull back the cocking bolt. He saw Auden come down to a kneeling position in what seemed to be mid-stride and the big gun come out and search for a target. 'No, you'll hit the –' He saw O'Yee skid to a halt beside Auden and shout something to him and then, almost in the same movement, gather Spencer in beside him and take aim with his revolver. Feiffer shouted, 'No! You'll hit Pak!'

He was babbling. Thirty feet away in the centre of the bridge, Pak was pressed down onto his knees with the long barrel digging into the back of his neck, pushing and pushing, searching for his life's centre. He was babbling. Pak, with his hands clapped across his face and his bladder going, yelled in Chinese, 'Help me! Save me!' He tried to twist his head up to see the source of the other voice at the end of the bridge, but he saw nothing. He was afraid to take his hands away. The gun was pushing hard on his neck. He heard it click in readiness. Pak, sobbing, yelled, 'Please! Please! *Save me!*'

'Let him go, Charlie!'

He saw Corey look up at him. The eyes were dead.

Feiffer, touching at his holstered gun, said, 'Charlie, let him go!'

There was nothing in the eyes. They were gone. They were dead sockets looking out from a skull. Feiffer, moving forward, yelled, 'Charlie!'

'Save me!'

'Charlie!!'

The eyes lit. For an instant, in the blackness of the skull, there was a pinpoint of light. It was reflected from the great overhead banks of illumination, fizzing and beating down with their heat from the warehouses. Feiffer, moving forward, said softly, 'Charlie, it's me! It's Harry! It's —' Behind him, he heard a movement. O'Yee's voice said to someone, 'Move off to the side of the building and —' and Feiffer half turning, yelled, 'No! Stay where you are!' He saw a tremor pass through Pak's body as The Far Away Man dug harder with the gun and then, as the gun moved up slightly on his neck —

Feiffer yelled, 'Charlie! Listen! Listen to me! *You know me!*'

The light was there. It was a pin prick in his eyes, but it was there. The Far Away Man said softly to someone, not to anyone on the bridge, 'Harry . . . ?'

Twenty feet from the bridge, O'Yee, pressing hard against Auden's shoulder, said in a whisper, 'That gun. Can you get a clean shot with it?'

Auden said, 'No. It's loaded with —' Auden, glancing around the warehouse and down to the footpath alongside the canal, said, 'Maybe if I —'

O'Yee said, 'All right, get around to the canal and if you can find something to rest it on —' His voice was carrying. Feiffer, turning, said, 'No! Stay where you are! That's an order!' He saw Pak begin to slump. He was going like a deflated balloon, sinking down from his shoulders as if he was melting, his hands still clamped over his face. He was making sobbing noises. He was dying. Moments were running out. Only the gun at the back of his neck held him up. Pak, taking one hand away from his eyes, said in Cantonese, 'Please . . . please . . . !' He was talking to shadows at the end of the bridge. He saw no one. Pak, staring, imploring, praying, said, 'Please! *Please!*'

'*Charlie!*'

There was a rifle in the back of the squad car. Spencer, glancing at Auden, said quickly, 'Christopher, I can go back and get the Remington —'

There was nowhere to shoot. Even from the side of the canal all the struts and supports of the bridge would be in the way. O'Yee, rubbing at his face and trying to think, said, 'No! Wait!' There was only room on the bridge for one. O'Yee, trying to see The Far Away Man through Feiffer's blocking body, said, 'No! Wait!'

Pak shrieked, '*Please!*'

'Harry?' The lights were all around him. He was on a bridge. He saw lights. Beneath him, in the canal, there were barges. He saw the lights and the habour and the barges. He —

The Far Away Man, shaking his head, said, trying to see him, 'Harry?' He saw the lights. The Far Away Man said, 'Harry, they killed everyone I loved,' He looked up for a moment, up high and above the bridge as if he was trying to look over it. He saw nothing. Whatever was there was gone.

Everyone he had ever loved had gone. One by one, in his life, one by one, they had all been taken away.

On the bridge, The Far Way Man said, 'Harry, they've all gone.' Behind him he could hear the lights fizzing and feel the heat on his back. Beneath him, under the bridge, there was the canal to the harbour. And the barges. He listened. He heard the water lapping against their sides. He listened. He heard the water. Behind him, the lights were fizzing and warming him. He thought he saw, just for an instant — There was someone crying and he thought just for a moment — The Far Away Man said, 'No.' It wasn't them. They were gone. The Far Away Man said –

'Let him go, Charlie!'

'What?' He was talking to the sounds and the shadows. He was listening. The Far Away Man, shaking his head, said softly to the sounds, 'No.' They were all gone now. The Far Away Man, looking down, said without pity to Pak, 'No, it's irrevocable.' There was no choice involved. The Far Away Man, talking to someone in a jade shop a long time ago, said in answer to a question, 'No, I don't have any doubts.' He thought, for an instant, that he saw the shadow again. The Far Away Man said softly, searching, 'Harry?'

It was not the same man. It was a corpse. He was unsweating, smooth, nothing but white bone and darkness where the eyes should have been. On the bridge, moving a step forward, Feiffer said softly, 'I know what happened, Charlie.' His eyes stayed on the glittering barrel of the gun. It was rigid and unmoving, digging into flesh. Feiffer said, 'Charlie, I've been to your apartment.' Behind him, there was a click as on the jetty someone did something with a gun. Feiffer, blocking the line of fire, said desperately, 'Charlie! *You could have come to me!*'

The Far Away Man said to the shadows and the sound of the water on the barges, 'No, I couldn't have done that.'

The eyes were gone and dead. There was nothing there. Feiffer, moving forward, said as an order, 'Charlie, we've got him now. Let him go.' He heard Pak make a sobbing sound. He was about to say something. Feiffer, over-riding him, said, 'Charlie, I know about the ship. I know what happened,' Behind him, he could hear O'Yee and Auden and Spencer. They were moving, going somewhere, setting up, getting their guns ready. Feiffer yelled, 'Charlie, *listen to me!*'

'Harry?'

The hair was coming out in clumps. He was no longer human. Feiffer seeing Pak tense, yelled at the man, 'Stay where you are! Don't move!' He heard something scrape on the jetty behind him. 'Christopher, keep everyone back!' Feiffer, taking a step forward, shouted, 'Charlie! Listen to me! I know what happened!'

'They died, Harry.' He was talking to the sounds in the water, to the sounds in the water and the barges and the bridge and the harbour a long time ago. The Far Away Man said, 'All of them. One by one. My father. You. My children. Carol. All of them.' He looked down. The gun was locked in his fingers. He only needed to take up the second pressure on the trigger. He heard Pak sobbing. The Far Away Man said, 'All of them, Harry, all of them. They all died.' He could not cry. He had no tears. The Far Away Man, shaking his head as if it was simply a piece of tragic information about someone else, said softly, 'There's no choice involved.' The man on his knees in front of him was something he had to do, something that had to be attended to because it was only right and proper and in the tragic telling of the events that had happened to someone else it was the only human reaction he could have been expected to have. The Far Away Man, cocking his head to one side for further instructions said suddenly, 'No!'

On the bridge Corey shouted, 'No! It happened to *me*!'

The gun came up.

Feiffer shouted, 'Don't kill him!' He heard a sound, then there was a glittering light on the bridge reflecting the lights of the warehouse banks. Feiffer yelled, 'For God's sake, Charlie, he's pissing himself in terror!' The Far Away Man's eyes were black sockets. Feiffer, touching at his own gun and gripping at its holstered butt for strength, yelled, 'Charlie! For God's sake, don't kill him!'

The eyes were glittering at him. They were bright with light and intensity. Feiffer, tensing with his hand still on his holstered gun, said pleadingly, 'Charlie, don't make me –'

'They all died, Harry!'

'I know.'

'They all died, Harry.'

Feiffer, moving forward, said evenly, 'Charlie, listen to me. If you kill him, you'll –'

'He's dead, Harry. He's already dead.' The Far Away Man,

making soft sobbing helpless sounds, said curiously, 'Don't you understand? You can't change something that's already happened! You can't bring people back!' He was shaking his head, pressing the gun harder into Pak's neck. Feiffer actually heard the trigger spring contract. The Far Away Man said, 'He's already dead! He was dead the moment they were!' His voice was going up, getting stronger, becoming unstoppable. The Far Away Man said, 'He's already dead! All that remains is for someone to actually kill him and make things the way they should be!'

'Like Shen and Sharwood and Mao and Oliviera?'

'Yes! Like them!' The Far Away Man said, 'Yes, yes! They were —'

The Far Away Man said, 'And him!' He jabbed hard at Pak's neck with the gun, 'And him! All of them!' The Far Away Man said, 'I was in Japan! I had one more job to do in Japan that was going to finish off my time with the company and then we were all going to —' The Far Away Man said suddenly, 'Do you remember the bridge, Harry? Do you remember the day you had to leave to go back?' The Far Away Man, talking to shadows, said softly, 'Harry, what they did to me — They —' There were no tears. The Far Away Man, hearing the sounds of the water and the whispers, said with remorse, 'I killed them all. This one's the last.' The Far Away Man said, suddenly smiling, 'Harry, we were boys together — well, at least, I was.' The Far Away Man, chuckling, said, 'Gilbert and Sullivan.' He shook his head. The Far Away Man said, 'Do you know which one? Aye? Do you?'

'No.'

The Far Away Man said, 'You do!'

'Charlie —'

'You do, damn it! It's from *Iolanthe*! It's from —' The Far Away Man said, 'You do know! You heard it at my house during the war! You do know!' He was shaking, trembling. The Far Away Man said, 'Shanghai! Who the hell in Australia during the war ever knew anyone who came from Shanghai?' The Far Away Man said, 'But I knew things too! I was important too!' He was shaking, the gun moving and pulsating in the light, 'I was – I was –' The Far Away Man said, 'During the war, when I – It made me someone, knowing you, having you in my house, being my friend! It made me someone!' Behind him, Feiffer heard O'Yee say, 'Christ, it's going to happen!' He heard a click. The Far Away Man said, 'I only came here because of you! To be like you! To see the places you'd seen – to be someone – to be important! To have something!'

'You had your wife and children!'

'Nikkie! One of my children was named Nikkie after your wife!'

'So what?'

'So nothing!' The Far Away Man said, 'So everything!' He looked down at Pak. 'I had everything right! I was going home! I had everything right and I was going home!' The glittering eyes came up. Time was running out. The Far Away Man said softly, 'I came here because of you, Harry, because of what you were.' He touched at his mouth with his free hand and looked down at the blood, 'And I –' The Far Away Man said sadly, 'And I got everything I wanted: I got Carol and the children and –' The Far Away Man said softly, 'And I was going home. I had everything I thought you ever had that made you better than me – that made me want you as my friend – and I was going home.' Beneath him, he heard the sound of the water against the hulls of the barges, 'They changed ships, Harry – while I was in Japan. At the last moment, while I was in Japan they changed ships.'

'Let him go, Charlie.'

'We all watched the *Straits Times* to see if it was ever reported but it – No.'

'Please, Charlie. It can't end well now.'

'Shen: the shoe shine man – he was the contact between them all: the messenger. I knew where he went on his beat. I knew he went to the jade shop first for the office workers and I knew –' The Far Away Man said, 'It was just like–'

'You could have come to me, Charlie! I tried to get in touch with you, but you –'

'No.' The Far Away Man, shaking his head, said, 'No, that wouldn't have been any good.'

Pak, saliva dribbling, said, '*Please!*' He was gone, jelly. Spittle was flowing down his chin and there was a white froth at the sides of his mouth. Pak, counting his last moments, said, 'Please! *Please!*'

'And Sharwood, Harry. He was the one who got the explosives. He was –' The Far Away Man said, 'I just walked in on him at the Club and I – and Mao: he was the one who told the Captain's fortune and sent him off course so that the rescuers would never find anything. Pak changed the sailing date to coincide with the fortune Mao had prepared. And Oliviera – he was the one who crated the thing on board, and, and– It went down somewhere miles off Malaysia.' The Far Away Man said, 'And Pak! He was the one who insured the ship so that –'

Feiffer said, 'And the cards were the proof that they were all in it together.' Feiffer gripping hard on the gun in his holster, said with sudden anger, 'You're not the only one who could have worked it out!' He took a step forward. 'Christ Almighty, did it have to come to this? We could have worked it out together!' Behind him there was a movement as Auden or Spencer or O'Yee took up position, 'God damn it, there are people waiting here to kill you! Don't you understand that? You could have come to me!' Feiffer moving forward, said, 'Charlie, for Christ's sake, I can look after you!'

'*No!!*'

'I can make it right! I can fix it!' Feiffer moving forward with his hand out to grab Pak, shouted, 'Charlie, for Christ's sake, you're out of your mind! Can't you even see that?' Pak was within six feet of him. Feiffer, moving forward, said evenly, 'Give it up, Charlie.'

'Will I get away with it, Harry?' The Far Away Man said, 'What about the other man I killed in the factory? The man from The Windjammer Club? Will I get away with that?' He looked down at Pak and decided to kill him now. The Far Away Man said sadly, 'No, no one ever gets away with what they do. I didn't. I did my best to be your friend – to be someone important to you – to be as exotic and strange and wonderful as you were, but I didn't get away with it. I was just thirteen years old and my father had been killed in the war and no one was ever coming back. Not you, not him – not my wife and children – not anyone.' The Far Away Man, squeezing at the trigger, said finally, 'No, you never get away with anything you do.' He saw a pulse beating in Pak's neck. The Far Away Man said, 'Never! You never do!' He looked up at Feiffer. He was only feet away. The Far Away Man said, 'Don't you understand? They're paying off on the insurance in the morning! I can't let them have it – they killed everyone I loved!' The Far Away Man, wrenching suddenly at Pak's shoulder and pulling his head up, shouted, 'Look at him! He's got the policy in his bloody pocket! He killed everyone I loved and he's got the fucking bloody policy in his pocket!' The Far Away Man shouted, 'All I ever wanted –'

'You wanted too much!' They were on the bridge again. It was a long time ago. Beneath that bridge, not on its way to war but to be scrapped, there was an American P38 Mustang fighter airplane. 'You always wanted more than people could give! God damn it, you've killed five people! That poor bastard the Factotum didn't have anything to do with this! You killed five people as if they were germs and you consoled yourself that they were nothing but –' Feiffer, reaching out for Pak, said, 'You're not killing anyone else! I'm not going to let you kill anyone else!'

'You could have found me if you'd really wanted to help!'

'I did try to find you! I went to your apartment a dozen times! I tried to ring you! I tried to –'

'You could have found me!' The Far Away Man, shrieking, said, 'In Australia, during the war –'

'We were kids! I wasn't anyone odd or rare or exotic. As far as I was concerned I was just me!' The Far Away Man was wavering. Feiffer saw the pressure come off the barrel of the gun against Pak's neck, 'You didn't want me as a friend! You wanted me as a possession!' Feiffer said, 'I know why you came here – to Hong Kong – you came here because I'd been here, because when we were kids it was something I had that you didn't! And then, when you'd got it, when you'd finally got what I had – Carol, your wife – she looked just like Nikkie – she even sounded the same!'

'It's not true!'

'It is fucking true!' Feiffer, only inches from Pak, shouted without mercy, 'And you're still doing it, aren't you? You haven't changed a bit! Shen, Sharwood, Mao, Oliviera and now Pak – they took something from you too, didn't they? Something you wanted, something you had to have, and now – and now you have to kill them, don't you? It isn't good enough to pass them over to someone else: to the bloody cops, because you – you have to own their punishment yourself!'

'*I'm dying, Harry!*'

Feiffer said, 'The final, ultimate, bloody possession. The last thing that's yours to dispose of . . .'

'They killed everyone I loved!'

'And the Factotum?'

'He was in the way!'

'In whose way?'

'In *my* way!'

'And what about me? I'm in your way now! What about me?' Feiffer, getting his hand onto Pak's shirt and twisting the material to get a purchase, said fiercely, 'But I want something now. I want something from *you*. You took everything you thought I had – and now it's my turn and I want this man's life!' He felt Pak's body quiver. Feiffer, pulling the man up to his feet, said fiercely, 'I'm calling in a debt, Charlie. You owe me and now it's pay-up time and I'm taking this man off the bridge because you owe it to me!'

'*You don't understand!*'

'Don't I?'

Corey said, '*NO!*' He was going, at the end. All his joints were hurting and he felt his knees giving way. His eyes were blurring and he felt the blood flowing freely on his chin from where his gums had shrunk with starvation and were breaking out in ulcerous sores and lesions. The Far Away Man said, 'No, I have to kill him! It has to end here – it has to!' His head was shaking backwards and forwards. 'It has to! *It has to end here!*'

'It isn't going to end here! I'm not going to let it end here!'

Behind him, O'Yee yelled, 'Phil!' The gun was moving away from Pak. It was moving up towards Feiffer. Auden yelled, 'I can't! I can't see to –'

'*Don't you understand?*' The gun was moving, glittering in the light. It was at full cock, the hammer straining against its sear, the first pressure on the trigger taken, only a hairsbreadth away from the liberation of the spring. The Far Away Man, moving the gun up, yelled, 'Harry, you promised! You promised!' The Far Away Man, reaching into his coat pocket with his free hand and pulling something out and holding it up, yelled, '*Look! Look!*'

In his hand there were two yellow cholera vaccination pages, both filled in in the same hand.

Feiffer, holding Pak, said softly, 'Oh my God . . .'

'It was me, Harry! It was my idea! It was my stake for Australia, my freedom! My –' The Far Away Man, crying, shouted, 'I insured the ship! It was me! It was all my idea!' The gun was at chest level. It was pointing at no one. There was no one else there. The Far Away Man, hearing the water and the sound it made against the barges, seeing the bright glittering Mustang so, so long ago, hearing sounds and voices and whispers, dying by degrees, yelled at the top of his voice to all the spirits of the dead, 'It was me! It was my idea! I was in Japan for an alibi when the ship went and I didn't know they'd change ships – I didn't know!' The Far Away Man, disintegrating before Feiffer's eyes, his face a contorted mask of irremedial agony, said, '*It was me!* I killed my own wife and children and – and everyone and –' The Far Away Man said suddenly, softly, 'Harry, it was *me!*'

The Far Away Man, alone on the bridge, the gun in his hand, said softly in a small child's voice, 'Harry, you promised . . .'

There were tears flowing.

The Far Away Man said, 'Harry . . .'

Harry, you promised . . .

The Far Away Man, raising the gun to his temple, said in a sad, soft voice, 'Oh, no . . .'

For a moment, he heard the sound of the water against the barges.

He was on a bridge, alone.

He heard, for a moment, the sound of his own voice a long, long time ago.

The Far Away Man, with no expression on his face other than a slight distortion about his eyes where the barrel of the gun pressed at his skin, said softly, 'Harry, if only . . .'

He was alone on the bridge.

It was such an easy thing to do.

'Harry . . . *wait*!'

Feiffer's hand was reaching out for him.

It was too far.

It was too long ago and too far.

'Harry, please . . . Please *wait* . . . !'

2.32 a.m.

Alone, on the bridge, The Far Away Man, sighing, his eyes full of tears, pressed hard, once, finally, at the trigger.

2.33 a.m.

Beneath the bridge, the water against the sides of the barges was lapping.

It was timeless.

It was a sound that knew, in memory or life, no cessation at all.

On the jetty by the great spice warehouses, O'Yee, glancing at Auden's face, said softly, 'Come on.' He looked to Feiffer with Pak on the bridge and Spencer, holstering his gun, going to him.

O'Yee, looking hard into Auden's face, said softly, 'Come on, Phil.' He thought of the guns.

O'Yee said, 'Come on, and if we can find anywhere open I'll buy you a bloody drink.'